"Why Do You Do It?"

she asked seriously. "You're bright, articulate, well educated. You could do almost anything you wanted for a living. Why do this?"

She half expected a flippant reply, or no reply at all. She was somewhat surprised when he answered, "I do it for the same reason you do, Teale." His tone was just as serious, just as matter-of-fact as hers had been. "There are dozens of other things you could do, just as there are for me. But none of them have quite the same appeal, do they? The glamour, the excitement, the danger, a new challenge every day. You and I aren't ordinary people, and we would never be satisfied living ordinary lives. That's why."

She drew a breath to protest, resenting the comparison and wanting to deny it was true. But she couldn't. He was right. But there was one small difference. They were on opposite sides of the law.

Dear Reader:

Welcome! You hold in your hand a Silhouette Desire—your ticket to a whole new world of reading pleasure.

A Silhouette Desire is a sensuous, contemporary romance about passions, problems and the ultimate power of love. It is about today's woman—intelligent, successful, giving—but it is also the story of a romance between two people who are strong enough to follow their own individual paths, yet strong enough to compromise, as well.

These books are written by, for and about every woman that you are—wife, mother, sister, lover, daughter, career woman. A Silhouette Desire heroine must face the same challenges, achieve the same successes, in her story as you do in your own life.

The Silhouette reader is not afraid to enjoy herself. She knows when to take things seriously and when to indulge in a fantasy world. Six books a month, Silhouette Desire strives to meet her many moods, but each book is always a compelling love story.

Make a commitment to romance—go wild with Silhouette Desire!

Best,

Isabel Swift
Senior Editor & Editorial Coordinator

DONNA CARLISLE
Under Cover

Silhouette Desire

Published by Silhouette Books New York

America's Publisher of Contemporary Romance

SILHOUETTE BOOKS
300 East 42nd St., New York, N.Y. 10017

ISBN: 0-373-05417-3

First Silhouette Books printing April 1988

America's Publisher of Contemporary Romance

Printed in the U.S.A.

DONNA CARLISLE

lives in Atlanta, Georgia, with her teenage daughter. Weekends and summers are spent in her rustic north Georgia cabin, where she enjoys hiking, painting and planning her next novel.

Donna has also written under the pseudonyms Rebecca Flanders and Leigh Bristol. *Under Cover* is her thirty-sixth book.

One

Teale Saunders knew three things for certain about David Carey: he was incredibly good looking, he was extremely wealthy and he was a criminal.

He was also, at this moment, smiling at her.

Teale felt just the smallest quiver of excitement—perhaps even nervousness—as she returned his smile coolly over the rim of her glass. The rumors about his mesmerizing effect on women had not been entirely unfounded.

"What do you think?" she murmured to Sam.

Sam, who had been surreptitiously watching the interchange, glanced at her as Carey turned casually back to his conversational group. "I think," he answered, absently swirling the liquid in his glass, "he's nibbling at the bait. And we've only been here ten minutes. Well done."

"Thanks," she replied. Her tone was dry, but she could not disguise the slight spark of triumph in her eyes as she looked around the room.

From the outside David Carey's home was no different from any other on the beach—neither pretentious nor modest, but standard beachfront fare that blended in comfortably with its neighbors. Subtlety was a necessary tool of David Carey's trade. The interior was discreetly decorated in shell beige and gray, with touches of turquoise that picked up the tones of the Atlantic Ocean, visible from three sides of the front room. To the casual observer, the house was indistinctive, and the party was no different from any other—unless, perhaps, it was quieter than some. It was only when one looked closely at the guests that one began to suspect this was no ordinary gathering of friends enjoying a sociable time on a Friday night.

The mode of dress ranged from tuxedoes to Hawaiian prints, from glittering gowns to cotton sundresses, but there was an aura of unmistakable elegance about it all. The ring worn by the woman in sandals and jeans was a flawless four-point diamond, the simple silk frock worn by her companion bore a Dior label. No one was in this room who could not afford to be, and all of them knew what they were here for.

The champagne was Dom Perignon, the caviar was beluga. The music was tasteful, and the conversation was punctuated by light laughter, the wink of jewels and the clink of glasses. David Carey circulated with the casual air of a genial host and occasionally would escort a guest or a couple into a short hallway and toward a back room. The door would close discreetly behind his chosen guests, and David would return to play host again.

It had taken three weeks to set up the invitation to this party, and Teale was excited. She enjoyed the glamour and the role playing, of course; one of the reasons she was so good at her job was that there were parts of it she found unabashedly fun. But mostly she enjoyed the challenge, the taste of victory after weeks of work, and yes, even the tiny edge of danger. For Teale wasn't particularly impressed by the size of the women's jewels or the vintage of the champagne. She was interested in what was going on in that back room.

Sam was eyeing the buffet table. "You want some shrimp?"

"Are you kidding? They're dripping in sauce, and this dress costs more than you and I both make in a month."

He grinned at her. "Perks of the job, sweetheart. You don't think the taxpayers would spring for a dry-cleaning bill?"

"I'm just not so sure how easy it's going to be to knock David Carey off his feet with shrimp sauce all over the front of my dress. And stop standing so close. He's looking at me again."

"It won't hurt him to think he's got a little competition." Sam watched the way she arched her neck to smooth back a strand of light red hair, and he watched David Carey watching. He frowned a little. "Maybe you're a little *too* good at this."

Teale hid her amusement by sipping from her glass. Sam and she had been partners for three years, and it was only natural that the closeness that developed between them on the job should spill over into their personal lives. Fortunately for their working relationship, each of them had decided at first glance that neither was the other's type. Sam was too short for Teale; Teale was too skinny for Sam. The resulting relationship was purely platonic, and if Sam occasionally carried his big-brother role too far, it was impossible to be seriously annoyed with him for it. He knew Teale too well to ever allow himself to become too overprotective.

"Getting to this party was one thing," Teale reminded Sam, watching David Carey from the corner of her eye. "Getting behind that door—" she nodded toward the hallway that lead to the back room "—is quite another. And that, my friend, is what you have me for."

Sam chuckled. "That's your problem, lady—no confidence. What makes you think he's going to take you back there the first time you meet?"

Teale gave a toss of her head, her hair rippling across her bare shoulders. "Because I'm good at my job."

Sam's eyes twinkled. "Are you sure you're in the right profession?"

Teale gave him a cool stare. "I'm just the cheese in the trap."

"Hmm." Sam cast his eyes to the side and then, casually, back to her. "You just be careful. That's a mighty big rat you're after, and he's moving this way." And, with a polite social smile and a nod, Sam sauntered off toward the buffet.

Teale felt a leap of her pulses, which she quickly subdued. She composed her features into an expression of casual boredom and gazed absently around the room, sipping her drink. She made certain not to look in David Carey's direction, though she could feel his approach much as she could feel static electricity in the air before a storm. Every nerve in her body was alert and alive. This was the moment she had been trained for, and she was ready.

"Miss Simon. You're looking neglected."

Teale Simon was the alias she adopted for all undercover work; it was simpler to remember a name that was close to her own. When David Carey spoke she turned slowly and favored him with a measuring smile. "How kind of you to notice, Mr. Carey."

He had greeted them at the door, of course, but that first meeting had been brief and impersonal, and Teale had been too busy checking out the room to pay much attention to her host. Now she had a chance to appraise him up close, and she was impressed.

He didn't look much like a hoodlum, she had to admit. He had a casual, easy-going air about him that suggested barbecues on the beach or touch football on someone's front lawn. He could have been a lawyer, a banker, a real-estate broker, and on first glance he seemed perfectly harmless. But Teale was trained to look beneath the obvious, to the thread of steel that wound beneath his lean, sexy frame, the trace of hardness just beneath the surface of his lazy gray eyes. Oh yes, he was dangerous. But perhaps not in the way she had first imagined.

His hair was sun-streaked brown, his eyes the color of smoked crystal. His skin was lightly bronzed by the sun; his features were sharp and aristocratic. Yet it was his mouth that immediately drew the eye and held the attention. His lips were distinctively etched, perfectly clefted in the center, flowing smoothly toward corners that could curve in a cynical smile or tighten with sternness or anger. It was a mouth an artist's brush

would yearn to capture and a woman's finger would
ache to trace. His was a striking face, an unforgettable face, filled with lazy sensuality and just a hint of
danger. It was a face even Teale, who was both fore-
warned and forearmed, could not help appreciating.

He was dressed fashionably in a safari suit with the
sleeves folded up above the elbows, a pale blue collarless shirt and casual loafers. But the suit was raw silk
and the loafers were Gucci, and he wore them all with
the negligent ease of a man who was accustomed to
having the best in life and never questioned his own
standards.

Expensive clothes, beachfront property, a sleek red
Porsche in the carport—thinking of how he had ac-
quired these luxuries caused a small knot of anger to
form in Teale's stomach, which she smoothly disguised with a smile.

"I was hoping you'd come over," she confessed. "I
really don't know anyone here, and there's nothing
more boring than trying to make small talk with people you're not interested in."

He lifted an eyebrow. "Shall I take that to mean
you're interested in me?"

It was not just his good looks that had earned him
his reputation of irresistibility with women, Teale realized, but something more subtle, less easily de-
fined. The gold-link bracelet he wore on his wrist, the
negligent way he held his glass, the casual stance he
took as he stood beside her, just a little too close—
watchful and relaxed, easy yet poised. It was in the
hint of knowing amusement behind those smoky eyes,
the faint curve of his lips, the lazy familiarity in his
gaze that he somehow managed to make seem comfortable rather than offensive. Much against her will,

Teale felt her pulses speed in response to that gaze, and she thought, God, he's good at this.

But then, so was she.

She swept him slowly from head to foot, and her smile deepened a fraction, invitingly. "Oh yes, Mr. Carey. Who wouldn't be?"

She could not be certain whether the amusement she saw in his eyes was gratification or mockery. She began to realize, to her annoyance, that it would never be easy to tell quite what David Carey was thinking by looking into his eyes.

But he responded gallantly, "I'm flattered, Miss Simon."

"Teale, please," she murmured, and he inclined his head in acknowledgement.

"And the gentleman you arrived with—" he nodded toward the buffet table without taking his eyes off Teale "—he wasn't, I hope, your husband—or boyfriend?"

"Sam?" She shrugged. "I barely know him. But he does get invited to some interesting places."

"And he brings some very interesting guests."

Teale was growing somewhat uncomfortable beneath his smiling, appraising stare. That lazy gaze was deceiving, for Teale suspected those eyes missed nothing. She tried to reassure herself that he would see nothing she did not wish him to see, but it was difficult to keep her uneasiness at bay.

Every detail of her appearance had been planned with painstaking detail and executed to perfection. The white strapless sheath she wore was classic and understated, woven with a tiny silver thread and fashioned in gentle lines that traced her hips and bosom as it dropped toward a subtly suggestive slit from calf to

ankle. The simple style was perfect for her, and the
color emphasized the golden tint to her skin and the
rich shimmer of her hair. The diamonds in her ears
were genuine—they had belonged to her mother—but
the one-carat pendant suspended from her neck had
been borrowed at great expense and under much du-
ress from the local jewelry store. She had brushed her
strawberry hair to a glossy sheen and allowed it to fall
over her shoulders, darkened her normally pale eyebrows and lashes, accentuated her usually non-
existent cheekbones with shadow and a sprinkle of
glitter, widened her eyes with a painstaking gradation
of subtle colors and brightened her lips with gloss. The
makeup job alone had taken over an hour.

Everything about her had been carefully arranged
to project negligent wealth and subtle good taste, and
she tried to assure herself her mask was perfect. But
beneath David Carey's probing gaze she felt like a
fraud. Did he see a woman who, without the elaborate costuming, was flat-chested, pale and plain? Did
he realize her perfectly manicured, ivory-coated nails
came from a box and the expensive scent she wore
from a tester bottle at the local department store? Did
he guess the dress was rented and the necklace borrowed?

And then an even more unsettling question oc-
curred to her: Would he care if he knew? Something
in the indulgent, amused expression in his eyes suggested he would not, and for a brief moment Teale felt
more like the mouse than the cheese. She did not like
that feeling at all.

She tilted her head to him and inquired, "Do you
always stare at people so, Mr. Carey?"

"Only beautiful women," he assured her.

Teale was not beautiful, and she knew it. She was tall and thin, with sharp features and a wide, expressive mouth. Her baby-fine hair was the palest of strawberry blonde, and she wore it long in a vain attempt to give it some appearance of fullness. Her complexion was the translucent porcelain common to most redheads, and her eyebrows and lashes were so light as to almost disappear against her skin. Without makeup, she looked plain and washed-out. With her most diligent efforts, she supposed she could look... unusual. Perhaps even striking. Apparently she looked unusual enough tonight to attract the attention of a man like David Carey, which was exactly what she had hoped for.

Still, she took his compliment with a grain of salt, and glanced appreciatively around. "There is a room full of beautiful women here."

He followed her gaze with an unabashed nod of approval. "So there is."

She looked at him speculatively. "I've heard you have a weakness for beautiful women."

"Did you now?" His eyes danced. "What else did you hear?"

She hesitated, then gave him a coy smile. Her blood was thrumming. "That you give very interesting parties."

He leaned toward her with the air of one imparting a confidence; at the same moment she felt the light touch of his hand upon her bare back. A totally involuntary thrill of electricity tingled her skin. "Actually," he confessed, "I find them an incredible bore. How would you like to rescue me from all this?"

The tip of his finger traced a little titillating pattern down the first three ridges of her spine, and that was

when Teale first began to suspect she was in over her
head. Her heart beat faster from nothing more than
his touch, and for just a moment, when her eyes met
his, she was totally at a loss for a response. Oh yes, he
was good. Too good.

She recovered herself quickly. "As a matter of
fact," she said brightly—perhaps too brightly—"I
would love a tour of your house."

He seemed to be watching her with more interest,
and it was all she could do to keep herself from blush-
ing under his scrutiny. His hand now rested in a light,
cupping embrace around her naked shoulder, and
though every instinct she possessed told her to move
away, she could hardly do that and keep up the role of
femme fatale she had determined to play. So she simply smiled up at him through a veil of lashes and pretended to enjoy it. She didn't have to pretend very
hard.

"It's a very ordinary house," he told her, and the
slight lift of the corner of his lips was both intimate
and inviting. "But the view of the beach is magnificent. Would you care to see it?"

For a moment she had a fantasy—walking along the
beach with him, the salt air riffling her hair, the damp
sand squishing between her toes...David Carey
draping his coat over her bare shoulders and, perhaps, taking her hand...warm skin, soft moonlight,
herself alone with this incredibly handsome and unmistakably exciting man....

Quickly, Teale took a sip of her drink, averting her
eyes for fear he might read the course of her thoughts.
What was the matter with her? She dealt in cold real-
ities, not fantasies, and this was no time for her to
forget that she was a professional. She gave an elabo-

rate shrug. "You've seen one beach, you've seen them all."

He laughed softly. "I feel the same way about houses." And, with a slight pressure on her shoulder, he started leading her toward the glass doors that opened onto the deck.

Out of the corner of her eye she saw Sam, a heaped-full plate in one hand and a highball glass in the other, his narrowed eyes telegraphing the message that he was ready to come to her rescue at a moment's notice. Something about that look rankled her and brought her clearly back to her sense of purpose. She did not need Sam's rescuing. She could handle this on her own.

And since subtle flirtation had gotten her nothing but trouble, she decided to take her chances with the direct approach. As they edged their way through the crowd she nodded casually toward the hallway that led to the back room. "What's going on back there?"

David gave her a speculative, slightly amused look and seemed uncertain whether to reply. Then his hand dropped to his waist and he replied, "An orgy, actually. Are you interested?"

"Thank you, no. The last orgy I attended was a dreadful bore. Perhaps if you had something more exciting to offer...?"

He regarded her for another moment with that thoughtful, humorous air, and then he murmured, "Perhaps I do at that." He turned and led her toward the hallway.

Teale's pulses were pounding with the taste of victory, and she could barely keep the elation from showing in her eyes. Not even the chief had believed they would gain access to the back room on the first night. But she had done it.

She caught a glimpse of the surprise and concern on Sam's face as they passed, and it was all she could do to keep from tossing him a look of triumph. Instead, she made a split-second gesture, a circle of her thumb and forefinger behind her back, and didn't glance at him again.

"Teale," David said as they moved into the relative quiet of the hall. "That's an unusual name." He paused and touched her chin with his forefinger, tipping her face up. The gesture took her so by surprise that she caught her breath.

He smiled. "I don't suppose there's any chance that you were named for the color of your eyes?"

He was very close, and her back was next to the wall. The subtle herbal scent of his cologne teased her nostrils, and his body warmth brushed against her. His eyes weren't entirely gray, she noticed then, but flecked with traces of midnight blue, like some exotic jewel. There was a light in his eyes that was rich with confidence and unmistakably sensual, and Teale began to wonder if she was really as clever as she thought.

Her breath was coming somewhat rapidly, and she could feel the heat that spread from the touch of his finger upward over her face. It was harder than it should have been to break away from the look in his eyes. It was very hard to keep her own eyes from straying to his lips, and Teale was ashamed of herself.

She was, after all, a professional. She said lightly, "You're very imaginative with your compliments, Mr. Carey."

His smile curved upward slowly, and he didn't move away. "Imagination, my dear Miss Simon, is the key to happiness."

Teale's heart was pounding hard, and she wasn't having very much luck keeping her own imagination under control. The man was a criminal. He dealt in vice. Who knew what really lay behind that door? And how could she be certain that the room he took her to was the room she really wanted to enter? Suddenly she wished her plan hadn't worked quite so well. She wished she had thought of another plan.

And then, casually, he dropped his hand and stepped away. "But I can tell you're not interested in philosophy at the moment. You were, as I recall, curious about the layout of my house. Tell me, Teale, are you a gambler?"

There, she thought. That's more like it. She relaxed cautiously. "I can be. There's a little bit of a gambler in all of us, don't you think?"

"Oh, without a doubt. What kind of games do you like to play?"

She met his eyes boldly and with just a trace of a provocative smile. "What kind are you offering?"

"Dangerous ones," he assured her. His eyes stayed with hers, just for a moment, as though in warning—or invitation. The cool calculation she saw in his face in that instant made her chest go tight.

And then he smiled and casually rested his hand on her back again, guiding her down the hall. He said, "I think I know just what you would like."

He turned the doorknob, and for a wild irrational moment Teale thought about the lady and the tiger. Then he swung the door open and ushered her inside.

Teale stood inside the doorway, dumbfounded. She had been so certain of what she would find that for a moment the images danced before her eyes like a mirage—the spinning roulette wheel, dice bouncing across green felt, stacks of crisp green bills being passed back and forth—but, of course, none of it was there. It was just a room. An ordinary room.

There were four or five people inside, watching television, playing pool or chatting amicably. There was a chessboard set up on a table and an array of video games and taped movies on the shelf. Three walls were soundproofed in silver carpet, and a fourth was covered by a poster-mural seascape. It was all so incredibly mundane that Teale, if she hadn't been so disappointed, would have laughed out loud.

She heard the soft click of the door behind her and turned to stare at David. Her disappointment must have been obvious, for he lifted an eyebrow in surprise. "What were you expecting—whips and chains?"

Teale took a breath. All right. So she had underestimated him. But the game wasn't lost yet.

She laughed lightly. "Really, Mr. Carey—"

"Why is it that I'm allowed to call you Teale and you call me Mr. Carey?" he interrupted smoothly, and came toward her.

She forced a dimple at the side of her mouth. "All right," she conceded, "David. And I must confess, this—" she made a vague, light gesture around the room "—isn't at all what I was expecting."

"I am so sorry." Deftly he plucked her glass out of her hand. "And your glass is empty, too. I'm turning into a terrible host, aren't I? George..." He turned in the direction of a small portable bar set up against the muraled wall. "Will you get Miss Simon some more champagne? I'll have another, too, I think."

The man who approached was the biggest, ugliest-looking man Teale had ever seen. His broad forehead and blunt, squashed-in features reminded Teale of a caricature of Frankenstein, and though she knew it was unkind, she couldn't help staring.

"George is my assistant," David explained pleasantly. "George, this is Teale Simon, our guest from out of town."

George took their glasses unsmilingly, and even though Teale made some uneasy effort to acknowledge the introduction, he turned away to refill the drinks with nothing more than a black stare that would have chilled the soul of a less courageous woman.

"Assistant?" remarked Teale. Mentally she corrected that to hit man. "What is it, exactly, you do?"

"A little of this, a little of that."

Teale had the impression he was deliberately goading her, and she bit down hard on her temper. After all, no one had told her this would be easy.

He led her to a plush velour sofa and gestured her to be seated. The deep, soft cushions almost swallowed her whole, and when he sat next to her he was so close she couldn't have inserted a piece of tissue between them. He rested his arm over the back of the sofa, and his presence seemed to engulf her—no, more accurately, to overwhelm her. She had to fold her hands in her lap like a schoolgirl to keep from touching him, and the soft, molding cushions made it impossible to inch away. Her discomfort, which she tried so hard to disguise, seemed to amuse David.

"And what about you?" he invited. Though he spoke in a normal tone of voice, there was an intimacy to the words, and she could feel his breath brush her cheek. "What do you do?"

Teale swallowed hard. Why should his mere closeness intimidate her so? He was just another crook. She met his eyes and replied deliberately, "A little of this, a little of that."

He smiled. "See how much we have in common?"

Teale was growing impatient, and that was a bad sign. She knew better than to rush a job like this. But David Carey was doing unlikely things to her judgment, and all that she had ever learned about pursuing a quarry seemed irrelevant in his case. Perhaps because she was beginning to have the uneasy feeling that she was the quarry and he was the one doing the pursuing.

In an unexpected movement, she shifted her position on the sofa, tucking one leg beneath her casually so that they were even closer than before. Her knee pressed into his thigh, and their faces were mere inches apart. As the crowning touch, she lifted her arm to the back of the sofa, too, resting it across his, her fingers just brushing his silk-clad shoulder. The flicker of surprise in David's eyes caused her enormous gratification, but she, too, was surprised by the pulse of excitement caused by the press of his thigh against her knee, the length of his muscles beneath her arm.

She said huskily, "Perhaps we don't have as much in common as you think, David."

His eyes flickered over her face and downward to her breasts, which were thrust into provocative prominence by her new position. That was, of course, exactly how she had expected him to react, but instead

of feeling powerful in her own womanly charms, Teale
felt strangely threatened, and she began to wonder if
she had gone too far.

His gaze moved back to her face. The subtle gleam
of sensuality there was hard to misread. "What makes
you say that, Teale?"

She gave a negligent turn of her wrist. "Oh, really,
David, you know why I'm here. Why everyone is here.
Let's stop playing games, shall we?"

His fingers clasped a few strands of her hair, twirl-
ing it gently, then letting it fall against her bare shoulder with a tickling motion. She tried not to shiver. "I
thought you liked games."

She managed a smile. "Video games? Pool? Chess?
I prefer something a little more stimulating. Something with—" she held his eyes meaningfully
"—higher stakes?"

His hand slipped beneath her hair, and his forefinger lightly traced the three cervical knobs—up and
down, up and down. This time she could not prevent
a spreading shiver, and her breathing quickened. A
slow light kindled in his eyes with her response. "The
stakes may be higher than you think," he said softly.

George chose that moment to arrive with the drinks,
and David had to remove his arm to accept them.
Teale, with a deep breath that was not entirely steady,
took that opportunity to resume her original position, leaning back against the corner of the sofa so
that he could not entrap her without being very obvious about it. And she, most certainly, would not try
that ploy again. She could still feel the tingle of fever
on the back of her neck where his finger had been.

Her smile was a little faint as she accepted her glass
of champagne; immediately she took a sip of the cool

tingling liquid, hoping it would help restore her equilibrium. It didn't.

What had gotten into her, anyway? David Carey was a lowlife criminal, and she was here to bust him, not seduce him. Somewhere in this house thousands—perhaps hundreds of thousands—of dollars were illegally changing hands. It was up to her to find out how and when and where. And given all that, why was she sitting here sipping champagne and playing word games with a man who was singlehandedly responsible for half the vice in this city?

David made no attempt to resume the closeness of his position, but leaned back against the cushions, one arm crooked casually over the back of the sofa, and sipped his drink. A good two feet separated them now, and Teale breathed easier.

"What are you drinking?" she remarked, for lack of anything better to say.

He tipped his glass a little. "Club soda." He smiled. "I don't drink. I don't smoke, either, or do drugs, or even overeat. As a matter of fact, for a man of my reputation, I have remarkably few vices."

Teale was certain that if she met his eyes at that moment he would have easily seen the contempt in hers. So she disguised her expression by sipping her champagne and letting her eyes wander over the room. The low drone of the television playing an old movie, the click of pool balls, the murmur of laughter... And then her gaze fell on the muraled wall, and suddenly she knew.

That was his secret room. That was where the real party was going on.

She brought her eyes back to him with a cool smile. "Oh, I think you have a few, David. The only thing I don't understand is why you're so shy about them."

His smile was lazy, but his eyes were alert. "If you're referring to my weakness for beautiful women, I don't consider that a vice."

This had gone on long enough. It was time to call his bluff. She said levelly, "You asked me if I was a gambler. I think you know I wouldn't be here if I weren't. And while I won't deny I've enjoyed our little...chat—" she made her lips twist upward in what she hoped was a coy smile "—what I'd really like to do is lose some money. Faro? Blackjack? People say you have the best dealers this side of Vegas."

His quiet smile did not waver. "Gambling is illegal in this state, Teale."

She gave a small sigh of exasperation, allowing her eyes to twinkle flirtatiously. "Really, David, you are the most impossible man. What does a person have to do to get invited to your infamous 'secret room'?"

He laughed softly, and Teale did not like that. She was almost certain it was gentle mockery she saw in his eyes. "Never on the first date, darling," he assured her.

Teale jerked her gaze away and had to take another sip of her champagne to compose herself. To get this close and fail. Teale Saunders never failed. She sighted her objective, she did her homework, she covered all the angles, and she did her job. It was as simple as that.

But she was beginning to suspect she had met her match in David Carey. And that infuriated her just enough to play her last, reckless card.

She gave an elaborate shrug and got to her feet. "Well, I must say I'm disappointed. I heard I could find some real action here, and that's the only reason I came. But if you don't think I'm good enough for your little games...."

He stood beside her, the smile in his eyes tender and appreciative. "Oh, I think you're good enough," he assured her softly, "for almost anything. And if it's action you're looking for..." He reached for her hand and held it with a warm and gentle pressure, his thumb tracing a light circular pattern over the pulse point on her wrist. Immediately, Teale felt that pulse speed. "Might I suggest a more thorough tour of my house? I'm sure that somewhere in all this we can find a place a little more private."

Teale's heart was beating fast, and her throat felt dry, and the gentle circular motion his thumb made against her wrist caused a prickling sensation that went all the way to the roof of her mouth. But she lifted her chin, she smiled at him distantly, and she replied, "Never on the first date, Mr. Carey."

The warmth of a gentle smile lit his eyes, and he lifted her hand toward his lips. "In that case—" his eyes never left hers "—I suggest we say good-night before we both get in over our heads."

Teale felt her breath catch as he turned her hand over and pressed a warm, lingering kiss against her palm. Electricity tingled in her stomach, and for just an instant the low drone of the television and the click of pool balls faded away, and she thought somewhat distractedly that she might already be in over her head.

"Good night—" David lifted his face, and there was no mistaking the gentle mocking laughter in his eyes this time "—Detective Saunders."

Two

A swarm of emotions swept through Teale just then—shock, outrage, incredulity. A cold clamminess seeped into her veins where fevered awareness had been a moment before. Then came fury and humiliation and, very far back, just the faintest edge of fear. What would a man like David Carey do once he had caught a cop trying to infiltrate his operation?

She stared at him, rapidly reviewing and rejecting options. She could try to brazen her way through; she could gather the cloak of her dignity about her and coolly deny any understanding of what he was talking about. She could, as long as her cover was blown and David seemed to be too distracted by his own amusement to expect anything of the sort from her, make a swift, forceful effort to enter the room behind the muraled wall. Or, more sensibly, she could turn and walk away with all possible haste.

In the end, however, she did none of those things. She simply withdrew her fingers, slowly and deliberately. She held his laughing gaze with no expression whatsoever in her own, and she inquired calmly, "How did you know?"

He appeared to consider whether or not to reply. "I'll tell you what," he decided at last. "I'll answer your question if you will answer one for me."

Teale said nothing. She didn't even blink.

He appeared to interpret her silence as assent and went on easily. "First of all, you were good—very good, in fact. I wanted to believe you, and that's half the battle with any role, isn't it? And of course—" he smiled indulgently "—you're a very sexy lady, which gives you an added advantage, as I'm sure you know. You might have been just a little bit too persistent, but I imagine most men would be too caught up in your charms to even notice."

A fine quiver of rage had begun within Teale from the beginning of his speech, and it was difficult to keep the angry tremor out of her voice. She was proud of the coolness of her tone as she interjected, "But you aren't most men."

He smiled—almost apologetically, Teale thought. "That's right. And that was your only mistake. The only thing I'm left to wonder is—" his eyes went over her, mildly, with an almost detached interest "—how far would you have gone to get your man?"

Teale turned on her heel and pulled open the door.

She strode down the hallway to the outer room, her color high and her eyes flaming. She didn't pause before Sam's startled, curious look; she didn't look back to where she was certain David Carey was standing, watching her departure with laughing eyes. She said flatly to Sam, "Let's get out of here. We've been made." And she kept on walking.

She felt Carey's humorous, thoughtful gaze following her all the way to the car.

By one o'clock in the morning, everyone had gone. The game room was closed down, the driveway was empty. The glasses and ashtrays had been washed; the money had been counted and locked away in the floor safe. David Carey's house was once again just another of a string of ordinary beach houses that dotted this part of the Atlantic.

David sat on the deck, a glass of club soda in his hand, gazing over the short expanse of sand-tufted lawn to the gentle rise and fall of midnight foam. He spent his most constructive hours just that way: gazing at the ever-changing face of the sea, listening to its whispers, thinking. The ocean after midnight never failed to soothe him, to challenge him, to inspire him.

The door opened behind him and closed softly; David did not look around. George walked over to the edge of the deck and took out a cigarette. The flare and sizzle of the match was a brief interruption to the night's stillness.

"You're going to kill yourself with those things one day," David commented absently.

George shrugged. "In our line of work, I don't really expect to live forever." He looked thoughtfully at the tip of the cigarette for a moment and added, "I'm not even sure I want to."

David took a sip of the soda. "What do you think?"

George looked out over the sea. "I think it's a hell of a mess." He took a drag on the cigarette and glanced at David. "How do you guess it happened?"

"Who knows? How do these things ever happen?" David was noticing the way the moonlight picked up odd gray-blue shadows at the edge of the horizon, and he suddenly realized where he had seen that color before. In Teale Saunders's eyes.

"What are you going to do?"

"I'm not sure yet." And he smiled a little, secretly. "You've got to admit, it's a challenge."

George grunted. "These kinds of challenges we can do without."

David chuckled. "You're growing soft in your old age, George. Challenges keep us on our toes. Always expect the unexpected."

George took another drag on the cigarette and crushed it under his foot, exhaling a stream of smoke with a weary sigh. He didn't look at David. "Do you want me to take care of the girl?"

David was silent, thinking it over. "No," he decided at last, slowly. "I'll handle it." And he got to his feet, smiling with the relief of a decision well-made. "Do you know, sometimes I really love this job."

"Calm down, Teale," Sam said wearily, for what must have been the tenth time. "It wasn't your fault. We were made before we ever walked into that room. Nobody's blaming you."

It was ten o'clock the next morning, and Teale had been pacing the floor of Captain Hollis's office for the past twenty-five minutes. Captain Hollis leaned back in his chair, absently glancing over the report, and

Sam sat on the edge of his desk. Both men waited patiently for Teale to wind herself down.

She stopped now before the door and turned, hands spread in a helpless, defiant gesture. "What I don't understand is how. *How* did it get out?" She shook her head adamantly. "No. I must have let something slip. I must have—"

"For Pete's sake, Teale, it was a setup, I tell you! That David Carey is one smart cookie, and we didn't check our backs, that's all. We walked right into it."

Teale ran an exasperated hand through her already-tangled bangs. "I should have known," she muttered. "A man like David Carey latching on to me when he had his pick of a dozen other women, pouring on the charm, oozing out the compliments. I should have suspected something right then. Hell, even three hours at the beauty parlor couldn't make me *that* irresistible!"

"So he goes for tall skinny redheads; there's no accounting for taste. Will you stop with the sackcloth and ashes already? You did your best. We both did."

But that was the trouble. Teale hadn't done her best. She'd let David Carey get to her; those smoky eyes, that slow smile, the tingling, insinuating caresses. She'd gotten too caught up in her own role. She'd started believing that she was an attractive, reckless woman out for nothing more than a good time and that David Carey could show it to her. She'd let herself be distracted, she'd lost the cool edge of detachment that was the mark of a professional. She had blown it, and she was furious with herself.

She walked over to the window and stood there, her hands on her hips, her brow drawn in a sharp frown as she stared sightlessly out. Sam, watching her, only shook his head and gave a sigh of exasperation.

There was very little resemblance between the woman who had stormed the office this morning and the willowy, sensuous creature Sam had escorted to David Carey's party last night. She was wearing slacks and a cream-colored blouse with long tight cuffs and flowing sleeves, and the color wasn't particularly flattering. Her pale hair was pulled back at the nape of her neck, and her feathery bangs were disarranged from the many times she had tugged at them during the morning. Her lipstick was gone and she wore no other makeup, which gave her face the pale, fragile look that could instantly arouse the protective instincts in a man. But appearances, as Sam well knew, were deceiving.

Teale Saunders had the delicate, defenseless look of a lost child. She wasn't pretty in a classical sense, but undeniably memorable. She could lure a man in with those big blue eyes before he knew what was happening and then devour him whole. Unfortunately, few people realized that beneath the innocent, vulnerable exterior lay a woman of steel until it was too late.

She turned abruptly from the window. "How?" Teale demanded again. "Will someone just please tell me how?"

"A dozen ways." Hollis spoke for the first time, barely glancing up from the folder. "A department leak, a snitch, word on the street, it doesn't matter. It's done."

Teale blew a breath through her teeth and began to pace again. Three weeks' work. One of the biggest operations they had had all year, gone. Just like that. She hated the thought of the wasted man-hours, she hated to lose the collar, she hated the prospect of David Carey's continuing his illegal operation untouched. But most of all she hated to fail.

She caught herself absently chewing her thumbnail and scowled again, folding her hands across her chest. Then the scowl deepened with thoughtfulness, and she turned slowly to Captain Hollis. "Listen," she said hesitantly. "I don't suppose—well, is there any chance we were wrong about him? Could Carey be innocent?"

The minute the words were out she knew they were foolish, and the patient, understanding look Hollis gave her made her flush. She didn't know where the thought had come from or what made her speak it out loud. Was she that desperate to soothe her own ego after blowing the assignment? Or was David Carey's innocuous charm still working its effect on her senses . . . and her sensibility?

Sam said flatly, "No way. You know that as well as I do. The man's got a record a mile long—"

"Our sources are impeccable," Hollis interrupted in that quiet, understated way of his. "And the very fact that he made you so quickly proves he's got connections of his own. And I can almost guarantee you they're not on this side of the law."

Teale knew that and was irritated that the Captain had had to point out to her so obvious a fact. What was she trying to prove, anyway?

Still, she felt compelled to correct Sam. "He doesn't exactly have a record a mile long. He's never been convicted of anything—"

"Because he never gets caught," pointed out Sam mildly. "The mark of a true professional."

"The man is running an illegal gambling house out of 628 Highland Lane," the captain stated flatly. "That much we know. What we need now—"

The door opened on the subdued clatter from the outer office, and the staff sergeant poked his head into the office. "Excuse me, Detective Saunders. There's a call on three I thought you might want to take." And at Teale's look of impatience he added, "It's David Carey." He closed the door.

Teale's eyes went from Sam to Captain Hollis, and she couldn't have said which was more acute at that moment—her astonishment or her curiosity. But when Captain Hollis silently pushed the telephone toward her and she picked up the receiver she knew exactly what she was feeling: excitement.

She said briskly into the mouthpiece, "Detective Saunders."

David Carey's smiling voice greeted her. "Good morning, Detective. I trust I'm not calling at a bad time."

Instantly, Teale had a vision of him clad only in a pair of swimming briefs or tight white shorts; his bronzed body stretched out on a deck chaise and glistening in the sun, a Bloody Mary dangling from his hand . . . no, she recalled, he didn't drink; make that a glass of orange juice. The surf dancing in the background, the beach beyond him dotted with gulls and early tourists, and David Carey, with dark glasses obscuring his eyes, looking sleek and sexy, smiling into the phone.

Her heart was beating fast, and there was a faint tinge of warmth all over her skin. She kept her voice perfectly expressionless as she replied, "What can I do for you, Mr. Carey?"

"I'm calling to apologize. I have a feeling I embarrassed you last night."

Embarrassed! Her eyes went wide with instant outrage, and only Sam's quick, curious look reminded her that she was conducting a business call, not a lover's quarrel. She swallowed her indignation and managed to return coolly, "That's quite all right, Mr. Carey. You were just doing your job."

He chuckled softly. "Oh-oh, you're still mad. You shouldn't take your work so seriously, Detective; I don't."

Teale's hand tightened on the phone. She was seething. "Unless there's a purpose to this call, I'm really quite busy—"

"Far be it from me to keep you off the trail of a desperate criminal. I was merely wondering if I might be allowed to make it up to you over dinner tonight."

Shock wiped out all other emotions. She turned to Captain Hollis, and she repeated blankly, "Dinner? Tonight?"

"Feel free to check with your supervisor," David invited easily. "I'll wait."

To Teale's consternation, Hollis gave a curt, decisive nod just then. Still, it took her a moment to regain her voice.

"As a matter of fact," she said into the receiver, "we do have some things to talk about. Dinner will be fine."

"Good. Do you know the Spindrift? About eight o'clock?"

Teale scribbled the name of the restaurant and the time on a notepad from the captain's desk. "That will be fine."

"Great. I'll see you then."

But she couldn't let it go at that. "Mr. Carey." She stared fixedly at the point of her pencil, poised above the pad. "Does this mean you've decided to cooperate with the police?"

His soft laughter caused her lips to tighten and her eyes to narrow. "Not a chance, Detective," he assured her. "Not a chance."

Teale replaced the receiver with quiet, deliberate control. She turned to Captain Hollis.

Two beats passed before Sam spoke up. "Since I don't really think you've taken to matchmaking for your detectives, Captain, my guess is the Carey case isn't closed."

Hollis said quietly, "Good guess." He opened the file again and gestured Teale to be seated. This time she did so without question.

"Carey is just the tip of the iceberg," Hollis said, after a moment. He glanced down at the file and then at his two detectives again, expressionlessly. "We let him slip through our fingers and we lose a lot more than one small-time racketeering operation; we lose the whole ball game. It's Carey's boss we're after. Gregory Diangelo. Drugs, prostitution, you name it, he's got it."

"And you expect Carey to lead me to Diangelo," Teale said slowly.

Hollis looked at her seriously. "At the moment, it's the only lead we've got."

Teale crossed her legs, lacing her fingers around one knee. Her expression was thoughtful. "Carey's pretty slick."

"And pretty damn confident," interjected Sam dourly. "Asking a police detective out to dinner. The man's either a fool or one of the smartest operators I've ever run across.''

Teale glanced at him. "He's not a fool."

Hollis said, "As far as we know, Carey's not dangerous. I wouldn't send you into this if I didn't think you could take care of yourself."

Teale nodded, but she was remembering smoky gray eyes and a slow smile. A small, involuntary shiver crept up her spine. She thought Captain Hollis should revise his definition of "dangerous."

She stood slowly, "So basically, my job is just to keep an eye on him and find out what I can."

Hollis nodded. "Think you can handle it?"

Teale smiled and hoped the gesture imparted more confidence than she felt. "Are you kidding? Spying is one of my best things."

Hollis picked up a pencil and began to make notes on the file, a sign that they were dismissed. Teale was at the door before he glanced up again. "Wear a wire," he said, and went back to his work.

The squad room was active and noisy with ringing telephones, clacking typewriters and uniformed officers moving back and forth. Teale found the purposeful routine a reassuring counterpoint to the daring, almost breathless course her thoughts were taking. David Carey. A second chance. David Carey, inviting her to dinner. What was he up to? And could she really handle it as well as she had led Captain Hollis to believe?

Sam followed her to her desk. "I don't guess I have to tell you I don't like this."

She sat down and began to sort through the papers on her desk. "Simple assignment, Sam."

"That guy is up to something, and you know it. You just don't call up and make a date with the cop who tried to bust you."

"'Tried' being the operative word," she answered dryly.

"Oh, for God's sake, here we go with the supercop bit again." Impatience tinged Sam's expression. "When are you going to learn that the fate of the free world doesn't rest solely in your hands? Everyone's allowed an off day once in a while, Saunders. What are you trying to prove, anyway?"

His words caught her off guard and stung more than they should have, more than Sam would have any way of guessing. What *was* she trying to prove? A lot, she thought bleakly, and then determinedly jerked her mind away from that course.

"I'm trying to prove," she returned lightly, "that David Carey is a small-time operative for a big-time crook named Gregory Diangelo and that both of them belong behind bars. Now, if you'll excuse me—" she tapped her copy of the Carey file with her fingernail "—I've got some studying to do."

"You just watch yourself tonight," Sam grumbled, as he pushed away from her desk. "And remember, I'll be listening to every sleazy word that high-priced Romeo whispers into your shell-like ear."

That made Teale laugh, but it was an uneasy laughter that faded the moment Sam was out of sight. Sam wasn't the only one who was worried. But what Sam was worried about and what Teale was worried about were two entirely different things.

Teale had come to Bretton Falls, South Carolina, three years ago fleeing scandal and shame and the dark turmoil of her own doubts. She had been looking for a quiet place to rest and lick her wounds. Bretton Falls was a medium-sized coastal resort town whose crime problems catered to the tourist trade—prostitution, minor drug peddling, the occasional gambling ring or property scam. Teale, with her excellent record from the Cleveland Police Department, had been more than welcome on the Bretton Falls force. No one had ever heard of her father here. No one knew why she had really left Cleveland. And no one, not even Sam, knew what she was running from.

She lost herself in her work because losing herself, right then, was exactly what she wanted to do. And because her work—the day-to-day battle of right against wrong, the good guys against the bad—was the only thing that made sense in a world that was constantly twisting and turning on itself. She was dedicated, she was ambitious, and she was driven. Her work was the only thing that mattered in her life. The only thing she could trust.

And it was for that reason that any small failure—real or imagined—bothered her so. What was she trying to prove? That she was good at her job, that was all. Or at least that's what she told herself.

She frowned and tried to concentrate on the file before her. She knew it all by heart. David Carey, alias David Carrington and Dave Hall. Age thirty-five, Harvard Business School graduate; his name at one time or another had been listed on the boards of directors of several businesses that were known fronts for laundering money. He had been orphaned at age twelve and taken in by a minor figure in the West Coast syndicate, Raphael Clealand, which had apparently paved the way for his future career. Clealand had been brought up on tax-evasion charges ten years ago but had died of natural causes before he was brought to trial. For the next five years Carey had kept a low profile, and little was known of him until he appeared in Florida connected with a numbers operation. He had slipped through the net on that one, and since then the story had been much the same—a string of bad connections and no convictions.

Teale found herself absently tapping her pencil on the edge of her desk, gazing at the file without seeing it. She was wondering why a man like that, with a superior education, all the worldly advantages, with such an abundance of charm and the obvious intelligence to elude the law for all these years—why a man like that would prefer a life of crime to the legitimate success that could have been his for the asking. Some inborn character defect, a traumatic childhood, an unresolved psychological problem?

She frowned irritably at herself. It was almost as though she were trying to find excuses for him, and there were none. What difference did it make why he had turned out the way he had? The reasons were immaterial; the fact was that David Carey *was* what he was, and it was her job to stop him. If she were looking for explanations for his behavior, a more pressing question was, why had he called her? Why would a man make a dinner date with a woman he knew was trying to arrest him? Was David Carey that reckless— or that cunning?

There was, of course, no point in worrying about it now. She would find out soon enough. Reluctantly she closed the Carey file and turned to more mundane paperwork. But she was aware of an irresistible excitement as she thought about the evening ahead, which was more than the ordinary nervous anticipation associated with her job, and she couldn't help reflecting on what a pity it was that a man as good-looking as David Carey should happen to be on the wrong side of the law.

Unlike David Carey and other enterprising professionals, Teale could not afford a house on the beach. Her apartment was on the outskirts of town, not more than six miles from the police department, but a twenty minute drive in the heavy, tourist-clogged traffic. She passed the sprawling resort hotel and its adjacent cottages, moved through the boardwalk area with its souvenir shacks and fast-food stands, and wound her way through throngs of sunburned families crossing the streets at will, laden with cotton candy, floppy straw hats, coolers and beach chairs.

Generally she enjoyed the sights and sounds of summer—corn dogs and suntan oil, carousel music and hard rock—and was amused by the little scenarios that were played out before her—the impatient mother dragging her children home from the beach, the teenage boys hanging out the car window while the bikini-clad object of their attention pretended utter indifference—but today she found herself experiencing an unusual amount of impatience, leaning on the horn at stoplights and wishing she had the time to ticket jaywalkers.

Her air conditioner had not worked all season, and the air in town was hot and sticky, thick with exhaust fumes. To make matters worse, her engine was beginning to overheat, and she had to lose her place in traffic to pull into a service station. "Whatever made me think small-town life would be quieter?" she muttered, and pushed her damp hair away from her fore-head as she got out to refill the radiator.

By the time she got home it was almost six-thirty. She was hot, sweaty and in a bad temper, and this was not a very auspicious beginning to the evening. What she really wanted to do was to sprawl out on the sofa and spend the evening sipping iced tea and watching television in quiet solitude. Had this been an ordinary date, she would have cancelled right then. But she was on duty.

She spent ten minutes standing under a tepid shower, letting the spray of the water drum away the grime and fatigue of a static day. Physically, she felt better, but nothing could soothe the nervous tension that was collecting in the pit of her stomach like a net full of heavy-winged butterflies.

What was she doing, anyway? What was Hollis thinking, making her agree to this? David Carey was not the kind of man to accidentally give them any-thing they could use; he was not about to take a mem-ber of the Bretton Falls Police Department into his confidence; he certainly was not going to slip up and lead them to Diangelo. No, David Carey was the type of man who would set up something like this just so he could laugh at the gullibility of the police force—or worse yet, use them for his own means. Hollis's entire plan, what little of it there was, was absurd. And Teale was doing nothing except walking into more humilia-tion.

She knew all this, but resentment and anxiety were background concerns. She stood before her closet for a long time, wrapped in a towel and biting her thumbnail. Mostly she was worried about what to wear.

The Spindrift was not a place Teale could afford to go on her own, and she consequently had very little in the way of appropriate dress to choose from. Last night David Carey had met a sleek, stylish woman in a designer gown and borrowed jewels. What would he think when he saw the real Teale Saunders—the one with stubby fingernails and limp, flyaway hair?

And what did it matter? Who, for heaven's sake, was she trying to impress?

Impatiently she jerked the first thing she saw off the hanger—a white linen suit with a black silk blouse. Good, she thought grimly as she stepped into the skirt. Businesslike, severe and totally unsuitable to a romantic rendezvous.

But the long-sleeved, high-necked blouse was much too hot for an evening whose forecast low temperature promised to be in the mid-seventies, and with the jacket it was stifling. At the last minute she changed the entire outfit for a square-necked, long-waisted sundress of blue-flowered polished cotton and didn't give a second thought to the fact that it was the most feminine thing she owned.

She applied a tracing of cover stick to hide the circles under her eyes caused by an angry sleepless night, brushed her lips with gloss and caught her hair back from her neck in a tortoiseshell comb clasp. She was halfway to the door when she remembered she had forgotten to put on the wire.

The microphone had been tested before she left the office. Sam, parked in a van across the street from the restaurant, would be able to hear everything that went on, and if she got into trouble help was only a few minutes away. In principle, it was the only sensible thing to do. In practice, it made Teale very uncomfortable to think of someone—even Sam—monitoring every word she said. Perhaps that was why she had almost forgotten to wear it.

By the time she had clipped the microphone to the inside of her bra and dressed again, it was a quarter to eight. "Oh well," she muttered, "it won't hurt him to wait a little." And then, more cheerfully, "Maybe he'll get tired of waiting and go home."

As she pulled into the parking lot, she saw the van discreetly parked in an alleyway across the street. "All right, Sam," she said, applying the parking brake, "ready for action." It was ten after eight, and the sun was just fading behind the tower of the Bretton Falls Resort.

Teale glanced in the rearview mirror to check her makeup, quickly blotting the dots of perspiration from her face with a tissue. She was glad she hadn't worn any mascara; it would be down her face by now.

She got out and locked the car door, and David Carey stepped up from behind her, his hand clasped firmly on her arm. "Good evening, Detective. I was beginning to think you'd changed your mind."

And, almost before she could react or knew what was happening, he had ushered her into the passenger seat of his car and locked the door.

Three

———

Teale didn't have to get into the car, of course. Once there she didn't have to stay. It would have been an easy matter to disengage his grip on her arm or to unlock the door and slide out as Carey came around to the driver's side, but Teale did neither of those things. She told herself that any dramatic attempt to escape would have been an overreaction to a situation that was, after all, still well in hand. But the truth was that from the moment he touched her arm she simply had not thought about doing anything else but following where he led.

He had disarmed her, and the fact irritated her. His smooth voice, his light touch, had caught her off guard and made her forget this wasn't just an ordinary date. He had gotten the upper hand, and that was not a very good start.

"Kidnapping, Mr. Carey?" she commented mildly as he slid behind the wheel. "I thought you tried to stay away from major felonies."

He tossed her a quick grin as he turned the key and revved the powerful engine of the Porsche. "Don't worry. I don't intend to take you over the state line."

"How reassuring," she murmured. In the side-view mirror, she saw the gray van ease toward the street, and then she was reassured.

"Seat belt, please," he reminded her, and Teale lifted a surprised eyebrow.

"Shall I take that to mean you don't intend to dispose of my body by driving over a cliff?"

"And waste a fifty-thousand-dollar automobile? Get serious."

He waited until she had secured her seat belt before he reached for a pair of glasses on the dashboard and put them on. They were prescription lenses, and Teale couldn't conceal her totally irrational surprise. "You wear glasses?"

"Only for driving." He cocked his head toward her innocently. "It's the law. Says so on my driver's license."

She stared at him. And so where was it written that a criminal couldn't wear glasses for driving? It simply seemed out of place, somehow.

He was dressed tonight in a shirt that was very near the pale-gold tone of his hair, cuffs folded up, collar undone. The lightweight material molded itself to the lean muscles of his arm when he moved, and the open top buttons revealed just the beginning of a light dusting of hair below the hollow of his throat. His khaki pants were clearly casual. He obviously had no intention of dining at the Spindrift tonight.

She inquired, for Sam's benefit as well as her own, "Where are we going?"

He rested his arm on the frame of the open window. The breeze billowed against his shirt and ruffled his hair. "Just some place a little more private."

She gave him a dry look. "Like an empty warehouse?"

He laughed. There was something unexpected about his laughter; she had noticed it last night, but today, dressed as he was with the wind in his hair and his eyes crinkling against the last dying rays of the sun, it was even more disarming. He laughed easily and naturally, without a trace of cynicism or bitterness, and it seemed unfair that a man as corrupt as he should find amusement so simple.

He said after a moment, "I wasn't sure you would come."

"That was a reasonable assumption." She turned in her seat a little to look at him, studying him frankly. "Why did you ask me?"

"Because," he answered without hesitation, "I like you."

She couldn't stifle the small sound of dry disbelief in her throat.

He glanced briefly at her, then back to the road. "I liked the way you handled yourself last night," he went on easily. "I liked the way your eyes flashed and your neck went pink when I found you out, but you kept your cool—that shows a lot of self-control. And I liked the way you played your hand, bluffing it through like a pro. And when you must have known you were in over your head, you threw caution to the wind and brazened it right out. Now, that's the mark of a true gambler. I like that."

"Coming from you, I suppose I should take that as a compliment."

"You should indeed. I told you we had a lot in common."

Teale gave a faint, mirthless smile. "And, of course, let's not forget your notorious weakness for beautiful women."

He glanced at her, and his smile was soft and appreciative and, to her very great surprise, held a hint of something that was almost genuine. "No. Let's not."

They turned onto the coastal highway, and Teale glanced again in the sideview mirror, looking for Sam. At the moment there was no sign of the gray van, but Sam could be just playing it safe. "Come on, Mr. Carey," she responded absently, her eye on the mirror, "if you expect me to believe a man like you regulates his life according to his hormones—"

"Of course not. Other factors must occasionally be taken into consideration. Don't worry," he added, following her gaze in the rearview mirror. "He's still there."

At that moment, the gray van rounded the corner three cars behind, and Teale jerked her eyes away from the mirror. She set her teeth against the flush of annoyance she could feel creeping up her neck. Damn the man, had he outguessed their every move? And what *was* he up to?

"Would you like to hear about the other factors?" he inquired politely.

"No," she said flatly. She turned again in her seat to face him, her expression determined and unamused. "What I'd like to do is call off the games, Carey. What do you want?"

He smiled. "What I want is to have a stimulating evening with a lady who interests me. What do you want?"

Teale drew a deliberate breath. "Right now," she muttered, "I think I want to go home."

He chuckled again. Teale couldn't help noticing how, as they drove into the dying sun, his eyes took on an almost crystalline character. "All right," he conceded. "You like things straight and up front; so do I. The fact of the matter is, you're an officer of the law and I'm a man you suspect of breaking that law. It stands to reason that you're not going to abandon the chase just because of a little setback like the one last night; by the same token it can't hurt me to keep an eye on you. We may as well make the time we would be forced to spend together as pleasant as possible, don't you think?"

She stared at him.

"Now tell the truth," he prompted, with a sly glance at her that seemed at the same time both sincere and flirtatious. "Wouldn't you rather be having a quiet, elegant dinner with me in some suitably atmospheric spot than sitting in a cramped car all night on a stake-out, eating cold pizza and drinking coffee?"

Teale wasn't certain whether it was incredulity or amusement that was bubbling to the surface, but she felt an almost irresistible urge to laugh. She subdued it with a slow shake of her head. "You are the most audacious man," she murmured.

He inclined his head modestly. "Thank you. Now, shall we just relax and enjoy the evening?"

This time Teale couldn't prevent a chuckle, and she settled back against the headrest. The funny thing was, she almost felt as though she *could* enjoy the evening.

And why shouldn't she? Everything was out in the open, and she had matters well in hand.

Besides, how many chances did a woman get to be wined and dined by an internationally known criminal?

She lifted an eyebrow as they turned off the highway, but made certain to keep her gaze away from the mirror. Sam could take care of himself. "Atmosphere?" she inquired. She knew of no restaurants or clubs this far up the beach.

"The best money can buy," he assured her, and then glanced at her with a grin. "Or perhaps I should say the best money *can't* buy. Some of the best things in life are still free, you know."

As the small side road began to loop in on itself, David pulled off and parked the car. On either side of them in the deepening twilight was a network of moss-draped trees giving way to a patchy trail of sand and sea grass that led toward the ocean. The puzzled amusement Teale had felt was lessened by a trace of alarm.

David got out and opened her door for her. "It's a short walk," he told her, extending his hand. And as she hesitated, he assured her, "Your partner is parked just around the bend. Nice cover, pleasant view. He'll be fine."

Teale scowled and refused his assistance as she climbed out of the car.

The sky had turned a deep, smooth shade of shadowed blue, but there was still enough light for Teale to make her way along the path without stumbling. David walked close to her, his hand so light upon her elbow that it was hardly a pressure at all, yet his presence was a rich and palpable thing. The scent of his cologne, the smooth grace of his stride, the brush of his fingers against her skin... awareness of him tingled down her spine.

They had gone less than a hundred steps when the trail opened onto a small clearing. To the right was a gradual descent toward the beach; to the left was a flat, perfectly formed bluff overlooking the sea. Teale caught her breath, staring.

"Well, for goodness' sake!" she exclaimed softly.

In the center of that small bluff was a linen-covered table set for two. Covered silver dishes and crystal glassware were shadowed by the twilight, and an ornate ice bucket held a cooling bottle of champagne.

For a moment she was too stunned to do anything but take it all in, then she gathered herself with a small, appreciative nod. "Not bad, Carey," she murmured.

David smiled. "And I thought you would be hard to impress."

She walked over to the table, wishing Sam could see her now. Imagining the expression on his face made her smile, and she suddenly felt an overwhelming sense of sheer pleasure for the entire episode. Who said undercover work didn't have its rewards?

David struck a match to the glass-globed candle in the center of the table. "Atmosphere," he pronounced. "And—" he removed the champagne bottle from the ice bucket and popped the cork with his thumbs "—elegance. Never say I don't keep my promises."

Teale watched appreciatively as he poured champagne into her glass, then club soda into his. "You sure know how to live, Carey," she commented wryly. "I'll give you that."

He handed a glass to her and lifted his own. His eyes were rich with subtle pleasure. "A toast," he suggested. "To a long and fruitful relationship."

Teale laughed and touched her glass to his. "That I can drink to."

She sipped the champagne, and the smile in David's eyes deepened as he watched her. For some reason that made Teale nervous, and she quickly averted her gaze.

"So—" she gestured around to include the bluff, the sea, and the elegant table setting "—do you do this sort of thing often?"

"As a matter of fact," he answered, "you've uncovered the romantic in me." He set his glass on the table and pulled out her chair. "This is one of my favorite spots. I've often thought how perfect it would be for a midnight picnic, but I've never done it before."

"Why not?"

"Because," he answered as she slipped into her chair, "I never found the right woman to bring here."

He let his hands linger for a moment on the back of her chair, and she found the simplicity of his tone, the softness of his smile, definitely disconcerting. She countered with a shrug and a dry smile of her own, reminding herself sternly that charm was David Carey's stock-in-trade.

"And naturally," she replied, "now that you've found the woman of your dreams, you've brought her here. I'm flattered."

He relaxed with a soft chuckle and went around to his own chair. "And what makes you think you're not the woman of my dreams?"

"Other than a slight conflict of interest—" she lifted her eyebrows "—nothing at all. After all, I'm legendary for my sirenlike beauty and devastating sex appeal."

David looked at her seriously across the flickering glow of the candle. "You don't think you are, do you?"

"What?"

"Beautiful."

Suddenly uncomfortable, Teale uncovered the dish before her to reveal an artfully arranged lobster salad. "Lobster, great. I'm starved."

"You're also evading the question."

"It's a stupid question." She picked up her fork and looked at him conversationally. "So. No parties tonight?"

He chuckled, acknowledging with a slight lift of his glass the change of subject. "Even crooks get a night off once in a while."

She speared a piece of lobster. "So, you admit you're a crook. Now we're getting somewhere."

"Would there be any point in denying it?" He lifted the covers on his own dish and took up his fork. "What about cops? I don't suppose you could be persuaded to take the night off?"

Teale slid the piece of lobster into her mouth and closed her eyes at the delectable flavor. She chewed, swallowed and gave David a sweet smile. "Not a chance."

The spark in his eyes was amused, and he turned to his own meal.

Teale had to give him credit, he certainly knew how to set a stage. The sea breeze ruffled the linen tablecloth and cast dancing shadows from the candle; the

ocean sighed and surged in the background, cresting
in dark peaks and milky foam. Vintage champagne,
lobster, etched crystal and heavy silver. The first few
stars were appearing in the deep navy sky, the taste of
salt was in the air. She felt the peaceful exhilaration of
being isolated at the top of the world with only the sky
and the sea for company. In Teale's life there was very
little room for romance, but she could appreciate it
when she saw it. And this was romance of the highest
caliber.

It was a pity it was just a game and that David Carey
was holding all the cards.

After a time David put down his fork and reached
forward to refill her champagne glass, which was almost empty. "Tell me about Teale Saunders," he invited. "How did you get into the Mata Hari
business?"

She chuckled. "Is that what I am?"

"To a point. And, as I may have mentioned last
night, you're not bad—for someone with so little experience."

She sipped her champagne. "Is that right? What
makes you think I'm inexperienced?"

He waved a dismissing hand. "I don't mean stalk-
ing and apprehending hardened criminals; I'm sure
you're quite competent at that. But you must know,
Teale, that a good undercover agent has to virtually
live his role, and there was something about your performance last night that didn't quite ring true."

Inwardly, she bristled, but she hid it behind a cool
"Indeed?"

"You allowed me to fluster you," he pointed out.
"Oh, not so much that it jeopardized the operation,

just enough so that I could tell you weren't entirely what you pretended to be."

Teale's muscles stiffened. She knew it. She knew it was her fault, she knew she had let something slip. But she had to ask, "Is that how you knew I was a cop?"

He smiled. "No. That's how I knew you were a woman who hadn't had many lovers."

She stared at him. She felt a slow flush creep up her neck, and the way his eyes moved toward it made her feel certain he was aware of it, though she told herself he couldn't possibly see anything of the sort in the candlelight. She took another sip of her champagne. "I hardly see what that—"

"But am I right?"

She thought of Sam, leaning back in the van, flipping through a magazine, munching on an apple, earphones in place. She said firmly, "This conversation is getting entirely too personal."

"Please. I'm trying to make a point."

She cast around for a diversionary tactic or a pithy retort, but it hardly seemed worth the trouble. In the end she gave an impatient lift of her shoulders and replied shortly, "In my line of work I don't exactly meet a lot of qualified candidates."

He gave a satisfied nod. "And you can't pretend to be something you're not—a seductress."

She gave a choked off laugh. "Well, I suppose I've heard worse insults." And she looked at him over the rim of her glass. "You, on the other hand, pretend very well."

He gave her a slow, rather vague smile, which had the effect of appearing both mysterious and oddly sad. "Don't believe everything you read in a wrap sheet, Detective."

She said, "Could I ask you something?"

He made a conciliatory gesture with his hand. With the candlelight softening his face and polishing his eyes it was difficult to remember who and what he was. It was difficult to remember to be careful.

"How did you make us last night? Was it something I did?"

He laughed softly. "Darling, I have sources that would put your own network to shame. I not only knew who you were two weeks ago, but when you were coming and exactly what your plan was."

Though that was hardly reassuring news, Teale couldn't help an enormous sense of relief. It hadn't been her fault. She wasn't to blame.

"Now answer something for me." He leaned back in his chair, his fingers absently stroking the stem of his glass, his expression easy and relaxed. "What constitutes a qualified candidate?"

The breeze ruffled his hair, and the candlelight played gentle, enchanting tricks with the soft upsweep of his mouth. His voice was soothing and mellifluous, and in some strange way seemed to invite confidence. Being with him, Teale reflected with a surprising lack of concern, was both stimulating and comfortable, like being with an old friend who never ceased to entertain, or growing relaxed in a new friendship...it was like being on a date. Or maybe it was just the champagne.

She shrugged and took another sip. "A lot of things."

"Just one. The most important qualification."

"Top of the list?" She met his eyes evenly over the rim of her glass. "Honesty."

He nodded soberly. "I can see how that would be a problem in your line of work."

"Not to mention yours."

His lips curved upward at the corner. "Touché." Then he grew thoughtful again. "I'll tell you what. Rather than spend the rest of our lives following in the footsteps of Diogenes searching for an honest man, let's you and I make a pact."

She lifted an eyebrow with interest.

"We can tell what lies we will to the rest of the world, but between you and I—honesty. It would be good, don't you think, to know at least one person from whom you can expect nothing but the truth?"

It must have been the champagne. She almost believed he was serious.

She said thoughtfully, "Complete honesty? All the time?"

He nodded, watching her.

"Do you think you're capable of it?"

"Without a doubt."

Her lips tightened at one corner. "Now the big question. Do you think *I'm* capable of it?"

"Oh yes," he said softly. "I think it's hard for you to be any other way. Which is one reason I was impressed by your performance last night—and also why I was so attracted to you."

Teale dropped her gaze, concentrating on gathering small droplets of moisture from her glass with her fingertips. Then she looked at him. "Are you running a gambling parlor out of your beach house?"

His eyes sparkled with amusement. "Really, Teale, why waste time with questions to which you already know the answer?"

"All right." Her gaze did not waver. "What's behind the sliding panel in your game room? The one covered by the mural."

He answered without hesitation, "Another room."

Her heart began to beat faster. She hadn't actually believed he would do it. She murmured, "That simple, huh?"

"That simple."

She took a breath. "What's inside the room?"

He laughed softly, shaking his head. "I really don't think you've quite captured the spirit of our agreement, Teale."

She liked the way he said her name. She had never considered her name pretty or poetic before, but when he said it, it seemed to be both. *Teale*. Like a caress.

There was a mixture of amusement and resignation as he met her patient gaze. "All right, fair is fair. But first, you must answer a question for me."

"We seem to be making a lot of bargains tonight."

"The sign of a good working relationship," he assured her.

She lifted her glass again. "Fair enough."

He looked at her frankly, but with a certain gentle curiosity far back in his eyes that should have warned her of what was to come. "Why don't you think you're beautiful?"

She had expected some probing inquiry into the details of the investigation, the hows and whens and wheres, or perhaps even some embarrassing but hardly lethal question about her performance last night. This caught her completely off guard, and for a moment she didn't know how to respond.

But after she had rearranged her slightly muddled thoughts, she was relieved. This was going to be easy after all. "Look at me," she answered with a slightly deprecating turn of her wrist. "I'm skinny, I'm pale, I'm plain. I have no eyebrows." She cocked her head toward him challengingly. "Do you think I'm beautiful? Remember the pact."

The feathering of lines around his eyes deepened with amusement, and he crossed one arm over his chest, cradling his glass in his hand, appearing to contemplate. His gaze went over her with thoroughness and deliberation: from her wind-ruffled hair to her candlelit eyes, resting for a moment on her lips then moving downward across her throat and the square of chest revealed by the sundress to the soft suggestion of her breasts, resting finally on her slender hands, crossed on the table near her champagne glass. She felt herself begin to glow beneath his gaze, as though it were his fingers, not his eyes, stroking her.

When he looked up his tone was serious. "No," he answered. "Not if by beauty you mean a hefty bosom and classic features and—" he smiled "—eyebrows. I've known a lot of women with eyebrows, and believe me, they're overrated."

She chuckled, and he went on, "Don't get me wrong. Last night you were stunning. In a room filled with beautiful women you stood out, but it wasn't because of the dress or the makeup or the jewels. It was the same thing that makes you even lovelier tonight, because you're *not* wearing any of those things. You're different. You don't need any props. And that, to me, is beautiful."

Teale swallowed hard on a suddenly dry throat. No one had ever said anything like that to her. There was a quivery feeling just below her breastbone, and she had to drop her gaze. "Well," was all she could manage.

He eased the moment with a charming, boyish grin. "What about me?" he invited playfully. "Do you like me, too?"

Teale laughed. What an incredible, unpredictable man. Everything about him made her feel alive and challenged, yet comfortable and familiar. She had never intended to have fun tonight. She knew she *shouldn't* be having fun. But she simply couldn't help it.

"I like your style," she told him, lifting her glass with a flourish.

"That's a start," he agreed, and he got to his feet gracefully. "And now, to top off an absolutely perfect evening, the pièce de résistance."

She lifted her eyes to him inquiringly as he held her chair. "I can't wait. A plane waiting to take us skydiving? A dozen tap dancers appearing from behind the rocks to sing 'New York, New York'? A jet ski to take us bounding across the midnight main?"

"Dull stuff," he scoffed. "I'm talking about something really exciting."

"I'm not sure my heart can stand it."

He smiled at her as she got to her feet. "We are going," he told her, "for a walk on the beach. And—" his eyes softened, oddly, as he tucked her arm through his "—I'm beginning to think it's my heart that's in danger, Detective Saunders."

Four

———

Teale thought, All right. Candlelight, champagne, sea breezes...you've had your fun. Now it's time to remember why you're here and get down to business.

The only trouble was, she wasn't sure she had ever known exactly why she was here. And with David's arm enfolding her own so protectively, with the lean strength of his muscle beneath her fingers and his warmth radiating gently against her side, it seemed less and less important to search for a reason.

He guided her carefully down the short path to the edge of the beach, and Teale bent to remove her sandals. The sand was cool and hard-packed beneath her feet, and what she wanted to do was simply walk, to let the breeze comb her hair and fill her with the quiet exhilaration that only a moonlit beach can produce, to link her hand with David's and inhale the salt air and listen to the surf and say nothing. To pretend—for just a little while—that she was falling in love.

The thought startled, even embarrassed her, and irritated her to the point that whatever romantic illusions had been formed by the night and the champagne fell away. She was here to do a *job*, for heaven's sake. Was she going to fail again?

Teale held her sandals negligently by the straps and absently grasped a shell from the sand with her toes while David removed his own shoes. She wondered if the microphone would carry this far over the sound of the surf.

"You didn't answer my question," she reminded David.

"Not yet," he agreed. He deposited his shoes and socks atop a rock and took her hand. It was such a natural gesture that Teale did not even think of objecting.

"Well?" she persisted, as they began walking.

"The question again?"

She frowned in annoyance. She might have known he would play his evasive games when it came to anything important. But she wasn't going to let him out of the noose that easily.

"What's inside your secret room?"

"It's not exactly a secret," he pointed out. "You know about it." And then, seeing the look in her eyes, he laughed softly. "All right, I'm sorry for teasing. We made a bargain and I'll stick to it, if for no other reason than to prove the theory that there's honor among thieves."

"Then prove it," she demanded impatiently. "What's in the room?"

"Card tables, chips, roulette wheels, slot machines," he replied with such negligent ease that it almost took her breath away. "A miniature casino, in fact, where almost any night of the week the rich and self-indulgent can lose fabulous amounts of money they won't even miss."

Sam, Teale thought on a surge of elation. Can you hear this? I did it!

David glanced at her. "I could take you there," he offered. "Tonight, or tomorrow night when the room is full of all sorts of people doing all sorts of moderately illegal things. You can see for yourself; you're welcome anytime. Of course—" he smiled "—by the time you returned with a search-and-seizure warrant, the room would be completely empty and I'd have two dozen witnesses to swear to the fact that there was never anything there but a storage closet. And by the way," he added casually, "in case you're wondering—the microphone you're wearing will carry back to your partner's van, unless of course the dampness causes condensation on the diaphragm, which sometimes happens with sea air. Police-department issue is often less than standard."

Teale pulled her hand away in contempt, her eyes sparking bitterly. "You enjoy this, don't you? Outwitting the law, toying with justice, crawling through the loopholes. It gives you a real boost to the ego to think you're outsmarting us all."

His expression was slightly apologetic, but greatly unconcerned. "It's the only way the game is played, Teale. You know that."

Yes, she knew that. The good guys against the bad, the same old story, time immemorial. And why should it bother her so much that David Carey was one of the bad guys?

She said sarcastically, "Next you'll be telling me that what I do for a living really isn't so different from what you do."

A spark of genuine mirth came into his eyes. "Is it? We both deal in deception, we both walk the edge between right and wrong—and we both enjoy it immensely. Sounds like more or less the same thing to me."

"The difference is," she retorted shortly, "I'm right and you're wrong!"

He tossed back his head and laughed. "Spoken like a true woman!"

She turned on him, her eyes blazing coldly. "That is utterly beside the point—"

He dropped his hands lightly onto her shoulders, startling her with his touch and with the gentle indulgence that replaced the mirth in his eyes. "It's a victimless crime, Teale," he explained simply. "I provide a service for which there is a ready market. No one gets hurt. Is it really worth all this fuss?"

"Yes," she replied stubbornly. "It's against the law, and you're a criminal."

Something crossed his eyes then that could have been a trace of nostalgia, and his smile seemed rather sad. "How good it must be," he said quietly, "to have everything laid out for you in black and white. Life isn't always that simple, Teale."

She pulled away from the touch of his hands, oddly disturbed. "It is for me," she replied shortly, and began walking again.

The breeze billowed and tugged at her skirt, shaping her legs and tangling her hair. David walked beside her silently, and after a while the lulling rhythm of the sea and the soundless pattern of their footsteps began to erode her anger and swallow it up. She didn't know why she had allowed him to upset her in the first place. She'd known what he was before she met him, and she should have known what to expect. She couldn't blame him for being himself.

They were walking near the tide line now, and the sand was warm and squishy beneath her feet. David, who was on her left, seemed oblivious to the fact that his cuffs were splotched with seawater. His hands were tucked into his pockets, his head tilted back slightly to catch the breeze or perhaps to count the stars. Teale, glancing at him askance, noticed the way the wind molded his loose trousers to the outline of his thighs, how his tousled hair seemed to catch stray rays of moonlight and how quiet and strong his face looked. A ripple of purely instinctive pleasure touched her as she watched him, and she was honest enough to recognize it for what it was. He might be on the wrong side of the law, she might be wary of him personally and despise him professionally, but he was undeniably one of the sexiest men she had ever seen.

He stopped suddenly and bent to scoop something up from the receding surf. When he turned and opened his cupped hand to her she saw he held a small, perfectly formed tulip shell. "A peace offering?" he suggested.

A reluctant smile dragged at the corners of her lips. "You think I'm that easily bought?"

"There are places in the world where shells are still used for barter," he informed her. "A shell like this would probably buy a man a week's worth of turtle meat or a strong, healthy wife."

A bubble of laughter escaped Teale.

"And look—" he stood close to her, and one slender finger traced the pattern of delicate violet against the translucent white shell "—this one is particularly rare. It's as smooth as pearl and as delicate as the color of your skin. And when I put it to my ear—" he did so "—I can hear the ocean, and it's sighing your name. Teale. . . ."

The exaggerated flattery made her smile, but there was a tenderness beneath the gentle, teasing light in his eyes, which caused her breath to still just for a moment. She tried to ignore the heaviness in her throat, the fluttering sensation just beneath her rib cage, but her voice was a little gruff as she replied, "Don't be silly. You can't hear the ocean in a shell like that."

"Listen," he said softly, and pressed the shell into her hand.

She heard nothing, of course. She saw nothing but David's face, the gentle curve of his lips, the absorbing light in his eyes. She felt nothing but his hand, cupping her face, his finger now tucking a loosened strand of hair behind her ear, now tracing a slow delicate pattern across her cheek. Her heart speeded, her breath was shallow, and she knew what he was thinking. It was the same thing she was thinking, and it was wrong.

She said, "David . . ."

"Shh. . . ." He removed his hand from her ear and placed his fingers lightly across her lips. Even as he did so, his head was moving closer, and then his fingers were replaced by his lips.

Even though she had expected it—even wanted it, secretly and shamefully, all evening—she wasn't prepared for the actual sensation of his kiss. Gentle, soft, moist ... yet shocking, electrifying, penetrating fibers and nerves that had long lain dormant, causing them to flare to life. She weakened and swayed against him. Her arms crept about his neck for support, and she felt the press of his fingers against her bare back. She parted her lips and tasted him.

She knew it was wrong. Perhaps it was that very wrongness, the touch of danger, the taste of the forbidden, which aroused her so. She only knew that when he kissed her the effect was like a match touching a volatile chemical—heat flared, and light blossomed upward in a rush of air.

He lifted his head slightly, and perhaps in that instant she should have twisted away. She could not. She felt his sharp inhalation of breath, saw the glow of passion in his eyes, then his lips had captured hers again, more powerfully this time, and she responded with equal abandon. His tongue touched her lips and probed the recesses of her mouth; her head spun. Her fingers cupped and pressed the muscles of his shoulder and his back; she felt heated flesh and silky fabric and the power of his heartbeat against her breast. She was feverish, she was trembling, she was helpless in his arms.

Then, abruptly, he broke away. The roar of her pulse left her dizzy. The small stifled moan she heard might have come from him or from her. He rested his chin on top of her head, and for a long time she remained cradled in his embrace, listening to the roar of the surf and the separate, echoing thunder of her own heartbeat, waiting for strength to return to her limbs and sanity to her senses. She heard the unsteady sound of his breathing and realized it matched her own.

At last she brought her hands to rest against his arms and, bracing herself, took a small step backward. David looked down at her, and he looked as dazed, as surprised, as she felt.

"Well," she said weakly.

He smiled. His eyes were busy, on her face, her hair, her lips. "Yes."

The salt air stung the fever on her cheeks, cooling it, and then he lifted his hand and touched her face, and she was afire again. He traced the shape of her eyebrows and her nose and her cheekbones, and when he touched her mouth her lips instinctively parted, tasting salt and roughness and male flesh. The pounding of her heart hurt her chest, and inside, the melting, liquid feeling began again. She tried to fight it.

"David."

His eyes were intent, alive, searching. He leaned forward and placed a light kiss upon her brow. "Your eyebrows are beautiful," he murmured.

His lips touched her cheek, his tongue flickered lightly along her earlobe. His lips dropped to her jawline, and when they touched her neck she arched to meet the caress. His fingertips stroked her shoulder, just beneath the strap of her sundress. She shivered.

He rested his face against her chest and breathed deeply. They stayed like that for a long time, holding each other, until heartbeats regulated again and breathing grew more normal. Teale knew she should step away, but she didn't. She wanted to hold him, to feel him, to revel in the aftermath of this dizzying pleasure for just a while longer.

"This could go further," David murmured at length, without straightening or loosening his embrace. "But—" she felt his smile curve against her skin "—I don't want to embarrass you. I think perhaps we should say good-night."

She looked at him uncertainly as he lifted his head and placed a light kiss upon her lips. "Good night, Teale."

He dropped another kiss onto her shoulder and then lowered his head and lightly, very lightly, kissed the curve of her breast, very near to where the microphone lay. "Good night, Sam," he said.

"This isn't going to work," Teale said firmly the next morning.

She stood before Captain Hollis's desk, her back straight, her feet planted solidly, an expression of formidable intractability on her face. Only her clenched fists betrayed the anxiety she felt inside.

Captain Hollis regarded her mildly, with an infuriating patience and a total lack of expression that compelled Teale to go on.

"He knows I'm a cop," she insisted, working hard to keep her voice calm and reasonable. "He knew I was wired. He knew he was being tailed, he even knew the exact position of the van every minute. This is hardly what I call undercover work, Captain. The man has been one step ahead of us from the beginning without even working up a sweat, and worse, he doesn't care."

Her voice was becoming more impassioned now, and she could feel angry color stain her cheeks—though whether the anger was generated by Captain Hollis's impassivity or David Carey's arrogance she couldn't be sure. "Nothing we do throws him," she said shortly. "Nothing *I* can do is going to trip him up, he's made that clear. What is the point of this operation, anyway? What can we possibly expect to accomplish at this point?''

She had run out of things to say. Captain Hollis simply continued to look at her, quietly, politely, without a trace of expression on his face to indicate what he might be thinking. From the outer office came the muted sounds of typewriters and ringing telephones, but the silence that emanated from Hollis's desk was thick and interminable.

At last he said, thoughtfully, "What do you suggest, Detective?''

"A surprise raid," she responded quickly, almost too eagerly. "We've surely got enough for a warrant, and we *know* we're going to find enough to put him away.''

Hollis nodded slowly. "How long have you worked vice, Saunders?''

Teale felt the flush, which had begun to fade away, creep up the back of her neck again. He knew that as well as she did. She had been transferred under his command. "Two years, sir.''

He nodded again. "Some things come with experience, I suppose. Like learning to look at the big picture and resisting the temptation to go for the quick fix. We can move on Carey tonight and put him out of the picture, that's true enough. Get him out of our hair, close the file, everything nice and neat, move right along to the next case, and maybe the next one won't give us so much trouble. But that's not really what law enforcement is all about, is it?''

She felt like a ten-year-old brought up before her school principal. She tried to brazen it out. "No sir, but—''

"Carey is just a symptom. We've got to try to cure the disease. And we're not going to do that by rushing in there with guns blazing like vigilantes in an old-time western."

"I realize that, Captain. But—"

"The object here is not to make life easy on ourselves, Saunders, and you know that as well as I do." His gaze became sharp. "Have you got a problem with this case you haven't told me about?"

Yes, she wanted to shout. *And every bit of it is on that tape Sam made of my dinner with David Carey last night.* A problem? She had a dozen problems. Smiling silver eyes, wind-tossed hair, a pact of truth. A man whose gentle probing questions made her want to bare her soul, whose kisses took her breath away. David Carey had already stripped her of her objectivity; what would he take next? *That* was a problem.

But she would admit none of that out loud. It was hard enough to admit it to herself. Let Captain Hollis believe the voice of the woman he had heard on last night's tape was that of one of his best detectives playing a well-rehearsed part; let him think she was just doing her job, let him think she had David Carey well in hand. Perhaps, if she worked hard enough at it, she would be able to convince herself of the same thing.

Teale drew a breath. "No," she said. "No problems."

He looked at her for a moment longer, and then gave a satisfied nod. "Good. Because I'm nowhere near to walking away from this case."

Then his tone became less brisk. "I know the odds seem stacked against us," he admitted. "It's a damned peculiar situation, and it's hard for an officer to know how to conduct an investigation like this. But there never were any hard-and-fast rules in undercover work; you know that. Almost every move you make is a judgment call. And I trust your judgment, Detective Saunders.''

Teale wished she had his faith. ''Thank you, Captain.''

''Right now the main thing we have to do is stay close to Carey. Something's getting ready to break, and we're never going to know what it is if we don't have a man—'' he almost smiled ''—woman in there. I know it may not seem like much, but right now you're the only lead we've got. Just hang in there and do your best.''

Teale mentally steeled herself. ''Does that mean you want me to actively pursue the contact?''

''I don't think you'll have to do that. Carey is a game player. He's getting a kick out of playing outsmart the cop, and his ego won't let it go. My guess is *he'll* pursue the contact. All you have to do is keep your eyes and ears open and wait. Chances are a man like that will trip over his own overconfidence sooner or later, and we'll be there to pick up the pieces.''

She nodded and even managed a semblance of her old cocky smile. ''Sounds simple enough to me.''

She turned to go, but Hollis called her back.

''Detective Saunders.'' His tone was serious. ''If any problems do develop, let me know. We can't afford to have you in there if your mind's not one hundred percent on the job.''

She hesitated and almost wavered. If she was ever going to get out, it should have been then, before she got in any deeper. But pride, stubbornness and professional integrity refused to let her admit defeat.

Or perhaps she, too, was suffering from overconfidence.

"No problems," she assured him, and left the office.

Outside, she took a deep, steadying breath and went over to her desk. So, that was it then. David Carey was her albatross—or she was his—for the duration. She tried to assess the positive factors. At least she knew where she stood with him; the lines were clearly drawn. There was no need for subterfuge—or at least, not much. He was pleasant company, amusing, even stimulating. The assignment would never be dull. And he found her attractive—or he pretended to—which should give her some sort of advantage.

On the negative side, she found him attractive, too, and that was no advantage at all. He *was* pleasant company—too pleasant. And too amusing and too stimulating for her own good. But perhaps the most disconcerting fact of all was the one that should have been the most reassuring: she didn't have to play a role with him. Teale had been playing roles all her life. Who was she supposed to be now that she was playing only herself?

Teale went through the telephone messages on her desk and didn't know whether she was relieved or disappointed that there was no message from David Carey. She entertained a brief hope that the captain might be wrong; perhaps Carey wouldn't pursue the contact after all. Immediately she dismissed the notion as pointless and futile. Damn it, she had a job to do. She was supposed to be going after the bad guys, not avoiding them. But everything about David Carey confused her, made her uncertain and hesitant to trust her own judgment. Such a state of mind, for a police officer, could unquestionably be dangerous.

Sam rested a sympathetic hand on her shoulder, rousing her from her troubled thoughts. For the first time in their association, Teale was not glad to see her partner.

"Saunders," he said soberly, "I admire you. How you kept a straight face through all that drivel he was dripping on you last night is beyond me. I about lost my lunch just listening to it."

Teale half thought Sam was serious, and that annoyed her. She avoided his eyes, busying herself with the papers on her desk, and replied shortly, "I've heard worse."

"Well, I guess lobster and champagne will cover a multitude of sins," Sam agreed philosophically, and that didn't help a bit.

Teale wondered what he had made of the long silences, the soft rustling noises that came over the microphone last night. Had he guessed David had kissed her—and that she had let him? Of course he had, she thought irritably, Sam was no fool. The question was, what did he make of it? He was certainly being very diplomatic, whatever he thought. And his tact, for some reason, annoyed Teale even more.

She looked Sam straight in the eye, and she said, "Let's stop tiptoeing around the subject, Sam. You know what went on last night."

"And you handled it like a pro," he assured her.

"That's *not* the kind of professional I'm trying to be," she flared at him, and he grinned.

"I've always said, being a vice cop is the best training in the world for real street work. Unemployment is not something you'll ever have to worry about."

Teale frowned, but she felt a little better now that the subject was out in the open. It was all part of the job, she assured herself. Sam knew that; she knew that. And they both also knew how difficult it was, sometimes, to tell where the job left off and real life began. Losing one's sense of perspective in undercover work was a constant threat and one she had been trained to avoid. She only hoped she had been trained well enough.

She picked up a pencil and tapped it thoughtfully against her cheek. She looked at Sam. "You're a man. What do you think was going on with Carey last night?"

Sam perched comfortably on the edge of her desk and replied without hesitation, "I think he's a man who knows a good thing when he sees it and doesn't waste any time going in for the kill."

Her expression turned dry. "How very perceptive. I don't suppose you'd care to be more specific?"

"All right," he answered frankly. "David Carey is an arrogant son of a bitch with the morals of an alleycat and about as much finesse."

"You just described every man I've ever known," Teale pointed out impatiently.

Sam's eyebrows flew up in mock indignation. "I beg your pardon. I thought you wanted my opinion."

"Please, go ahead. Maybe I should take notes."

"Quite aside from the fact that you could pick up lines like his in any bar in the city at half the price," Sam went on intrepidly, "he has all the markings of a sociopath—"

"Oh, come on, Sam! Don't you think that's going a bit far?"

"—in that," Sam continued deliberately, "in his particular area of expertise—which is deception, fraud and evasion—he not only shows no sign whatsoever of conscience, but actually enjoys making things difficult for himself. The hotter the game, the more he wants to play. And a man who courts danger that closely has got to be just a little bit dangerous himself. That's what I think."

Sociopath? Dangerous? Teale didn't like what Sam thought at all. And because she didn't want to think about how close Sam might be to being right, she deftly returned the ball to Sam's court. "All right, hotshot. You seem to have it pretty well figured out. What would you do if you were me?"

Sam appeared to give this some consideration. "Well," he replied at last, "I wouldn't kiss him, that's for sure."

Teale scowled at him, but in fact she was relieved. She'd been waiting for a gibe like that all morning, and now that it was out of the way she could relax. Sam wasn't one to push his luck.

"I think," she replied, giving him a cold stare, "the first step is to get rid of the wire."

"Suits me. If I had to listen to any more of that garbage, I'd be unfit for duty. But the Captain might have a thing or two to say about that."

Teale could well imagine he would, but she didn't consider the matter open for negotiation. The woman in her rebelled against undergoing another humiliation like last night's, while the practical, professional side of her insisted that if she were going to go through with this, she may as well do it right. It was obvious she would get nothing more from David Carey until he trusted her, and he would never trust her as long as a hidden microphone monitored his every word.

She began to absently chew on the end of the pencil, trying to formulate a plan—trying, somehow, to get a grip on a situation that was already beginning to slip out of her control. "The shortest route between point A and point B..." she murmured out loud.

"Is a straight line." Sam leaned forward and took the pencil out of her hand. "Lead poisoning," he pointed out politely.

"That's an old wives' tale."

"What straight line are you trying to follow?"

"Diangelo. He's the object of the entire investigation, isn't he? David Carey is just window dressing, and the time we spend on him is traveling in circles and corkscrews rather than going straight to the source." Even to herself that sounded like rationalization, just another way to get out of a job she didn't want to do. But she was grasping at straws now.

"Maybe," Sam admitted reluctantly. "But right now Carey is the straightest line we've got. And you, my dear detective, are a straight line to Carey."

"Well, so far that's gotten us exactly nowhere." Her tone was challenging. "Have you got a suggestion?"

"I do." Sam got to his feet and pushed casually away from the desk. "You've got a pact of truth with the man, don't you?" He grinned. "Ask him."

Teale's features drew into a formidable scowl as he sauntered away, but it wasn't Sam's flippancy that angered her, it was the fact that it might work. And that possibility made her very uneasy.

Which was, of course, ridiculous. Was she to accept the word of a man like David Carey? Did she believe that he could have feelings, whimsies, sincerities and pleasures like an ordinary man? Did she believe that he thought she was beautiful? Did she believe that stunned, pleasured look in his eyes after he had kissed her? And most of all, did she really believe that he had meant it when he promised her nothing but the truth between them?

Far away, some small treacherous voice deep inside her whispered, *Yes...* Yes, in some strange way a part of her almost did believe all of those things. And if he lied—which, if she asked him about Diangelo, he was certain to do—she didn't want to know about it. She was perfectly aware that that was both perverse and unprofessional, but she simply wasn't ready to confront David Carey on the subject of his veracity.

What she did want to do was find out as much as she could about him. That, in fact, was the only sensible thing she could do at this point—and the only thing she could think of to keep from going crazy waiting for him to call her. There were big gaps in the police file that made Teale uncomfortable, and a great many things she needed to know for herself about Carey's connections in town. And *those* were things she could do something about.

With a surge of energy, she whipped the cover off her typewriter and set to work, busying herself with useful, productive, positive things: sending off requests for information to various government and local agencies, making phone calls, dragging Sam along for firsthand interviews with contacts who might be able to provide something the police didn't already know. It would take several weeks to get a reply to any of her letters, the phone calls proved fruitless, and the

interviews were entertaining but hardly enlightening.
But for the remainder of the day Teale hardly thought
about a kiss on a moonlit beach.

Five

Teale asked very little from life. A place to lay her head at night, a square meal at least once a day—and an automobile that worked. After spending the day lost in the fast-paced world of high-level crime fighting, it was somewhat of a letdown, to say the least, to find herself standing by the side of the road sweltering in the six o'clock heat and staring at a steaming engine.

Cars swept by in a roar of exhaust fumes, causing Teale to shield her face against the dust and the taste of carbon monoxide. "Blasted tourists," she muttered, which was almost a blasphemy in itself, since eighty percent of Bretton Falls's economy—and at least fifty percent of Teale's job—was dependent on tourism.

She slammed the hood closed and walked around the car. The nearest phone booth was conveniently located at the nearest service station, about two miles back, and standing in the hot sun swearing at her car wasn't getting her any closer to either one. She reached inside the car and jerked her keys out of the ignition, slung her purse over her shoulder and slammed the car door. She didn't bother to lock it. With any luck, an auto thief would stop by while she was gone and solve the entire problem.

She'd walked fifty yards when she heard a car slow down and pull to the shoulder behind her. Somehow she wasn't in the least surprised when she turned and saw a sleek red sports car idling patiently at the side of the road, and she didn't even have to guess who the driver was.

Teale's heart was beating fast as she walked slowly toward the car, but she told herself that was only from the heat. She came around to the passenger side, away from the traffic, and bent down to the window.

"Car trouble?" inquired David Carey with a grin.

She answered dryly, "I don't suppose this is a co-incidence?"

"I never leave anything to chance, my dear. I followed you, of course. And lucky for you I did."

"You're a mechanic?"

"Not on your life," he replied cheerfully, "But I won't charge you for the ride home." He popped the lock on the door, and when she hesitated he lifted an inquiring eyebrow. "Unless, of course, you'd rather walk?"

Teale opened the door and slid into the rich leather upholstery. There was something very annoying about accepting a ride in a car that cost more than her annual net salary while her own pathetic bucket of bolts stood wheezing at the side of the road, but she tried to be gracious. "Nice car."

He cast her a laughing look. "Who says crime doesn't pay?"

Teale took a deep breath, which she hoped he did not notice. So, here she was. It was one thing to spend the day resigning herself to her assignment and to the fact that she would be forced to see David again; it was quite another to actually do it. Too many emotions were bouncing back and forth in her head. How was she supposed to feel, how was she supposed to act? Did he really expect her to pretend as though last night had never happened and continue with their semi-professional adversarial relationship? Was that even possible? Or perhaps what he was expecting was just the opposite. After last night, perhaps he no longer considered her his adversary.

Well, if that were the case, it was up to her to point out his error in judgment without delay.

Absently, Teale pushed her perspiration-soaked bangs away from her forehead, and David, noticing the gesture, raised the windows with a touch of a button. In an instant, cool air flowed over her face from the air-conditioning vents.

"Rough day at the office?" he inquired solicitously.

She smiled sweetly. "No more than usual when I'm in hot pursuit of a dangerous felon."

"And the dangerous felon would be—"

"You."

"Wrong," he pointed out. "I'm not a felon, and I'm not dangerous. However, I do like the idea of being the object of a hot pursuit." He paused. "What did you find out?"

She laughed.

He slanted her a quick crooked grin. "Just checking."

Dimly Teale heard the alarm bells go off in the back of her mind. There it was again: the charm, the easy laughter, the feeling of being comfortable around him. The way he leaned back in the seat, one hand casually guiding the wheel, his light hair ruffled and his eyes shaded by tinted driving glasses.... For goodness' sake, why was it so difficult to think vicious thoughts about a man who wore glasses?

He was wearing a bright blue T-shirt, white duck pants and deck shoes, and the clothes only added to her sense of disorientation. She preferred him as she had first seen him at the party, smooth and sophisticated in high-fashion raw silk, holding a glass in his hand, regarding her with cool amused eyes from across a room filled with strangers. Then he had looked like just what he was, a high-powered operator with a taste for luxury and the illegal means for satisfying that taste. Today—even last night—he looked almost ordinary. Except, of course, that he was still better looking than any ordinary man she had ever known.

David signaled a turn and pulled into a service station. "They should be able to tow your car from here. What's the problem, do you know? Water pump?"

Teale shrugged. "Old age, ill health and a general decline. The hazards of a low, low sticker price."

David looked at her sympathetically. "It sounds like you should seriously consider upgrading your lifestyle."

"And I suppose you know just the way to do it," she returned dryly.

He grinned. "Don't knock it if you haven't tried it."
He opened the door. "Sit tight where it's cool. I'll take
care of everything."

Teale didn't like the genuine temptation she felt to
just sit back and let David take care of everything, so
she made herself leave the luxury of the air-
conditioned car and follow him into the greasy-
smelling service station. She listened in quiet amazement while he briskly described the location of her
automobile and the probable cause of the problem,
gave her license number and proceeded to leave ex-
plicit instructions for what he wanted done when the
car was towed in. But when he reached for his wallet
Teale pushed ahead of him, plopping her credit card
down on the counter with a stern look for David.

"I take it you don't like the take-charge type," he
murmured.

"You take it correctly."

He nodded, as though in agreement. "I can understand that, I suppose. You must get tired of men
wanting to take care of you, but it's not really our
fault. You look so small and fragile it's only natural to
assume you need taking care of. The male protective
instinct, you know."

Her withering look told him explicitly what she
thought of that assumption, but in case he missed the
point, she said, "Most people only make that mistake
once, Carey."

"I'll remember that."

She signed the charge slip, and he touched her
shoulder lightly as they walked back to his car. Even
that innocent, meaningless brush of his hand against
her shoulder brought back too-poignant memories of
last night, making her skin heat briefly before she

sternly regained control of herself. A job, Teale, she reminded herself. It's only a job. But just how much was she expected to endure for the sake of duty?

"I don't suppose I have to give you my address," she said as they got back into the car.

"Now what kind of bad guy would I be if I hadn't already cased the joint?" And, when she didn't smile, he added, "How would you like to have dinner first? In a real restaurant this time, if you like."

"Thank you, I have other plans."

"Which means you left your hidden microphone at the office."

"Bad planning on my part."

"Does that mean you're officially off duty?"

She shot him a meaningful glance. "I'm *never* off duty."

"And I thought *I* had bad hours," he murmured.

Teale turned to look out the window in order to disguise a smile. Damn, but he was hard to resist. The moment she had convinced herself to despise him—or at the very least, to regard him as nothing more than another lowly suspect—he did something to make her smile or draw her into an exchange of wits or make her forget who she was and who he was.

And perhaps that was the entire problem. The line between duty and desire was becoming too easily blurred, and Detective Saunders was slipping too often into Teale, the woman. That had never happened to her before. The lines of demarcation had always been clearly drawn; she never allowed her personal life to encroach upon her professional one nor vice versa. She had always known exactly who she was and what her job was. But with David...

She knew her job. She had him, as it were, under surveillance. She had him in the car with her. She had, to a certain extent, his confidence.

So why didn't she ask him about Diangelo?

Her gaze happened to rest upon his hand as it lay on the steering wheel. It was strong and lean, the fingers slender and long and lightly tanned. Her gaze moved to his wrist, with its sprinkling of pale hairs, and along the length of his forearm. She watched the way the muscles flexed slightly as he turned the wheel, lengthening and relaxing, and she remembered how his arms had felt around her last night, how his hands had felt, pressing her back, cupping her waist.

And then she knew very clearly where duty ended. She had stepped over the thin line that separated the law officer from the woman the moment she had allowed him to take her in his arms last night, and she didn't want to make that mistake again.

But she was afraid the damage had already been done.

She pulled her gaze away from him and cleared her throat, which had suddenly grown dry. "That's it, up ahead."

"I know." He made a turn into the neatly landscaped apartment complex and gave her a smile that made her heart beat faster. Deliberately, she looked away.

"So," he inquired, "what's on the agenda for tonight?"

"A cool shower, a tuna sandwich and the Alfred Hitchcock festival on Channel 39."

"No kidding? That's exactly what I had planned."

"I'll just bet."

He pulled his car into an empty parking space in front of her building. Teale's hand was on the door-handle before the car came to a complete stop.

"Thank you for the ride, Mr. Carey," she said briskly. "I hope we'll meet again under more formal circumstances—your trial, perhaps?"

He turned to her, resting an arm across the wheel, as she opened the door. "You're not going to, uh..." He made a gesture toward her apartment.

She smiled coolly as she got out. "No, I'm not going to invite you in. Good night."

"I'm disappointed in you, Detective," he said sadly. "This is a flagrant disregard of your duty. What would your superior say?"

He couldn't have picked a more unfortunate time to be right. She *was* neglecting her duty. Her assignment was to keep an eye on Carey, to foster their relationship. He had provided her with the perfect opportunity and she was walking away. Captain Hollis would be shocked. *She* was shocked. And she took it out on David.

She stood before the open door, looking down at him, for just another moment. Then she said simply, "My job description does not include entertaining suspects. Nor does it include romantic candlelit dinners, long walks on the beach, listening to cheap pickup lines or physical contact, except when making an arrest. It most certainly does not include heartfelt tête-à-têtes or long soulful kisses. So if you will excuse me—" she smiled politely "—I'm hot and tired and I've had a hard day. Besides, I've just decided I *am* off duty, after all."

She slammed the car door and walked to her apartment, holding a satisfied picture in her mind's eye of

the look on David Carey's face. For once, she had had
the last word.

For the first time all day she was at ease with herself concerning David Carey. She knew what she had
done tonight was no permanent solution, nor was it
probably the wisest course of action—in fact, she was
certain there were repercussions yet to come—but for
now, it felt good. She'd bought time to fall back and
regroup; later, she would plan a new strategy.

She felt renewed as she stepped out of the shower
and let the cool stream from the air-conditioning vents
dry her skin. She stepped into a pair of shorts, put on
a halter top and pulled her wet hair into a ponytail
without bothering to dry it. She left the bedroom with
nothing but tuna fish and Alfred Hitchcok on her
mind.

David Carey was sitting on her sofa, casually
watching the evening news. "There's a tropical
depression off the coast of North Carolina," he said
in greeting. "Looks like we might be in for a storm."

For a moment Teale was rooted to the spot with rage
and indignation. But before the anger even peaked, it
faded into simple resignation. Sometimes there was
just no point in fighting the inevitable, and the truth
was that she had a job to do. She couldn't avoid it, she
couldn't ignore it; David Carey was here and the decision was taken out of her hands.

And on the heels of that acceptance came another
realization: she was glad. She should have been furious, dismayed and resentful, and to a certain extent
she was all those things. But when she came into the
room and saw him sitting back on her sofa, lean and
lanky and relaxed and looking so perfectly at home, a

tingling anticipation began within her that she couldn't explain and didn't even want to try to understand. He filled the room and brought it to life, and everything within her responded to his presence.

She didn't know whether that was good or bad. But she was fairly certain it had nothing whatsoever to do with her job.

He stood and let his gaze travel slowly over her sparsely clad figure. Her skin prickled with his gaze, but she faced him in stony silence.

He gestured toward the door. "You left your door unlocked," he explained.

She said nothing.

He took a step toward her, and there was something in his expression that intrigued her—sincerity mixed with a trace of uncertainty. She'd never seen him look uncertain before and hadn't thought he was capable of it.

"Look," he said quietly, "I won't stay. But I couldn't leave you with the wrong impression about what happened last night. You can accuse me of a lot of things, and you'd be right about most of them. But I wasn't using you last night. It started out as a game; we both knew the rules. But the things I said to you I said to Teale the woman, not the cop, and I meant them. When I kissed you, I did it because I wanted to. If you want to know the absolute truth, it took me by surprise."

The way his eyes flickered over her lips, then back to her eyes again brought a rush of memories—his taste and texture, his warmth and power. For an instant she relived the dizziness, the rush of pulses, the blind sensation, and she thought, *Oh, yes. It was good, it was real. And it took me by surprise, too....*

The moment between them suddenly seemed poignant and electric, bridged by memories neither could control, and Teale was glad that he was the first to break the eye contact. A half smile crooked his lips as he finished, "Of course, if I were smart it might occur to me to wonder who was really using who last night. I notice you're not making any claims about your own motives."

That rankled—which was, perhaps, exactly what he wanted. "I don't owe you any explanations, Carey," she said sharply. "And I'd appreciate it if you would stop treating our relationship like a blind date. I—"

"Relationship?" he interjected with a lift of his eyebrow. "Well, that's a start, anyway."

"You humiliated me," she said quietly, "in front of my co-workers and my supervisors. You knew damn well that everything you said or did last night was being monitored and recorded—"

"So did you," he pointed out mildly.

"You made me look like a fool! Worse yet, you plotted it from start to finish. Now you expect me to believe this drivel about your sincere intentions—"

His eyes flashed with brief sharp anger, and that startled her. "Now you wait just a minute," he said coldly. "It's not drivel. If I wanted to feed you a line, I could come up with one better than that. I've got more respect for your intelligence than that; I certainly hope you have more respect for mine."

She took a breath, momentarily uncertain. The anger in his eyes and the tone of his voice caught her off guard. He didn't look like a smooth con artist anymore. He looked like . . . a rejected suitor.

"I don't like being used," she said forcefully. "Especially not by you, and especially not—"

"Sexually?" he finished for her, and Teale's color flared. She clamped her mouth shut.

David released a slow breath. "Look," he said, with deliberate calmness. "I wasn't using you. Not then, not now. I don't *have* to, don't you understand that?"

Teale remained stubbornly silent. She had gone too far already. What was the matter with her, arguing with a suspect? What good did she possibly think it would do?

But a part of her was unwillingly intrigued, and she made no move to end the discussion. She wanted to hear what else David had to say.

"You have nothing I want," he explained patiently, as though it really mattered to him that she understand. "I have no motive to lie to you or deceive you or try to seduce you. Whatever information you might have, I can get a lot quicker and more easily from another source—as I've already proven. I'm not stupid enough to think that if I make love to you you're going to drop the case. In fact, it's just the opposite. If the department suspects you're getting personally involved they'll pull you off the case and assign someone else and what good would that do me? As a matter of fact, *I'm* the one taking all the risks here, and you're the only one who has anything to gain."

Reluctantly, she had to admit that made a certain kind of twisted sense. What *did* he have to gain by a kiss along a moonlit beach? Except the obvious, of course.

He must have seen a flicker of concession in her eyes, because he continued, more gently, "The plain fact is, unless you asked to be transferred from the case, we are going to see each other again. There's nothing I can do about that. The other fact is that I'm attracted to you." His lips curved downward in a smile that was both self-mocking and endearing. "And there's nothing I can do about that. What I can do, however, is keep my hands to myself, if that's what you want. As you pointed out, a man like me doesn't allow his life to be ruled by his hormones. I'm sorry you misinterpreted what happened last night, and I'm sorry it made you uncomfortable. It doesn't have to happen again."

She stared at him. What an incredible man. She didn't believe a word he said, of course, but ... what an incredible man.

He hesitated, as though waiting for her response. Then he glanced toward the door. "Well. That's all I wanted to say. I was with you last night because I wanted to be, and I'm here tonight for the same reason. But I can see the feeling isn't mutual, so I'll leave."

It said something for Teale's powers of recuperation that he was halfway to the door before she said, "Wait." And it said even more for her state of mind that, even as she spoke, she didn't know why she had called him back.

He turned.

She didn't believe him, not for a minute. This was nothing more than another facet of his renowned charm, just another trick to catch her off guard. She assured herself of this, she acknowledged that she knew perfectly well what she was getting into and was entirely capable of handling it. She said casually, "You don't have to leave."

He came back over to her slowly, a questioning look in his eyes. "Does this mean you believe me?"

She looked at him thoughtfully. "No," she answered. "It means I have a job to do. And I just went
back on duty."

"Pity. I just went off duty."

He smiled at her, and she found herself smiling
back, and she thought helplessly, Who are you kidding? You believe him. She didn't want to, she tried
not to, but for just that moment she believed everything he said was true. And though she knew it was
foolish, it made her feel good to believe.

"Shall we start over?" he suggested. "Would you
like me to go outside and knock on your door and
pretend the last ten minutes never happened?"

She shook her head. "No," she said seriously. "I
think we do too much pretending as it is."

Something in his eyes deepened, as though in approval, or even tenderness, and he touched her arm
lightly. "Good for you," he said softly.

She felt her heart begin to speed, though whether it
was from his touch or that entrancing light in his eyes
she couldn't be sure. She turned quickly toward the
kitchen. "Do you like tuna?"

"Next to lobster, my very favorite seafood," he assured her, following.

His gaze moved around the room and he commented, "You have an interesting apartment, Teale.
Not at all like what I expected."

Teale decorated with extravagant use of colors—in-
dulging her love of rich tones and bright colors in her
decorating scheme to compensate for the blandness of
her wardrobe. Her own pale coloring would have been
overwhelmed by the bright oranges, yellows and blues
she adored had she worn them, but in her apartment
she gave herself full rein. Her decorating scheme had

been called absurd, blinding, startling and—by the less tactful—hideous. She thought "interesting" was a mild way of putting it.

Her sofa was covered in a brilliant blue-and-red Indian print, the carpet was daffodil yellow. One wall was painted fire red and hung with abstract prints in violet and yellow. A whimsical orange rocking chair dominated one corner, and an array of oversize rainbow-colored cushions were scattered along the walls. The windows were lined with bright blue sheers beneath drapes of a bold red-and-white print. The end tables were covered with paisley scarves; shadowboxes and wall shelves held an eclectic array of collectibles: paperback books, records, glass miniatures, ginger jars and odds and ends from twenty-eight years of living. A cuckoo clock that didn't keep time was displayed on one wall, next to a framed cover from an 1899 Sears-Roebuck catalog. Whatever she valued, she displayed, and that was why she was somewhat disconcerted when David noticed the seashell he'd given her the night before sitting on the shelf next to a photograph of her parents on their wedding day.

To distract him, she said, "It's just an ordinary apartment. What did you expect, Miami Vice?"

He turned the shell over in his hand, smiled and replaced it. "Something like that."

"Not on the Bretton Falls Police Department budget." She vowed to get rid of that seashell at the first possible opportunity. She didn't know why she had brought it home in the first place.

But she did know why she'd saved it, and she also knew she wasn't going to throw it away. Not yet.

He picked up the photograph. "Are these your parents?"

"Yes," she said shortly. "Don't snoop. I didn't go prying into your private things when I was at your house."

He laughed. "The hell you didn't! You only tried to take my house apart room by room." She frowned in irritation, and he added, "Besides, you've seen how I live. It's like a hotel room. There's nothing there to pry into. Your place is like a treasure trove."

"Or an attic." She went into the kitchen, leaving him to follow or not as he pleased.

"Exactly. Full of clutter and color and a thousand stories. Remember, I told you it was hard for you to be less than honest? This apartment proves it. Everything you've ever thought or been is written all over the walls."

That assessment made her somewhat uncomfortable, though she suspected it was true. Her professional life was structured, regimented and too often fraught with secrecy and deception. Her home was the only place she could express herself freely, and she did it with a passion. What disturbed her was the fact that David recognized that so easily, and that, in a single glance, he'd learned more about her than she wanted anyone to know.

She took a can of tuna from the cabinet and applied the electric can opener to it. "Do you always make such a big deal out of things?" she inquired, somewhat irritably.

David leaned against a counter. "Only things that interest me. And, as I may have mentioned before, you interest me."

"I'm flattered."

She went to the refrigerator and took out mayonnaise, celery and onions. When she turned to close the

refrigerator door with her elbow, David was in front
of her, very close. She didn't know why that startled
her. Perhaps it was a sudden awareness of the
strangeness of the domestic scene—David Carey, here
in her kitchen, politely relieving her of a jar of mayonnaise and a bunch of celery, preparing to dine on
tuna fish and ginger ale after last evening's feast of
lobster and champagne. Perhaps it was the fact that he
looked as comfortable here as he had over an elegant
candlelit table, and just as natural. Perhaps it was
simple awareness of him, his tanned forearms, his flat
abdomen, his lean thighs, the brush of his hand
against hers as he took the celery from her and the
warm, fleeting scent of his cologne. She felt the small
hairs on her arms prickle with his closeness, and she
turned quickly away.

"Would you like to know what it is about you that
interests me?" David placed the celery and mayonnaise on the counter beside her.

"Pickles," she said.

"Not even close."

"No. I forgot the pickles." She started to turn back
to the refrigerator, but he held up a hand.

"Allow me."

Teale stretched overhead for a mixing bowl and she
didn't have to glance around to know that David was
watching. She was too acutely aware of how sparsely
she was dressed, of how her torso was exposed and her
breasts thrust forward as she lifted her arms. The
awareness was both discomfiting and strangely exciting, just as it would be to any woman who knows she
is being watched by a man, and who likes it.

The refrigerator door opened and closed, and David placed a jar of pickles on the counter with the rest

of the ingredients. "Do you want to know?" he repeated.

"No."

His tone was reproving. "I thought we were going to be honest."

She sighed. "All right. Tell me, why do I interest you?" She broke off a stalk of celery and began chopping.

"That's it." He smiled. "You have ethics. When you make a pact you stick to it and you don't cheat. You haven't, for example, asked me about Diangelo."

Everything within her stopped. Her hand paused in its chopping, her breath caught in midinhalation, her heart skipped a beat. She heard the refrigerator motor click on and a car door slam outside, but inside everything was suspended.

But it was only for an instant. Her heartbeat resumed at an increased pace, her mind started working with the same heightened rapidity. She resumed chopping the vegetables, and she inquired casually, "Would that be cheating?"

"Yes, it would. Because under the terms of our agreement, I would have to answer you honestly."

All right, she thought. Everything inside her seemed to be working double time. Her thoughts were racing, and adrenaline was flowing. Even her stomach was jumping as doubt warred with certainty, reluctance with determination. *It's worth a shot!*

She put down the knife; she turned to face him. She hadn't realized how close he was standing until just that moment. When she turned, her shoulder almost brushed his chest. For some reason, that only made her heart beat faster.

She looked up at him. She asked calmly, almost casually, "If I did ask you, what would you say?"

He looked at her soberly. "I'd say," he answered, "stay away from him."

His eyes were slate-colored, heavy with things she couldn't read. She could see the slow rise and fall of his chest and the beginnings of his beard stubbling his chin. "He's bad news, Teale, and you're about to get in over your head. I'd tell you to back off, for your sake and mine."

Slowly, he lifted his hand and touched a damp strand of her hair that had strayed over her forehead. His voice had a husky texture, deep with sincerity. His eyes were fixed on hers, seeming to try to probe into the very depths of her mind. "I would say that you're about to make a big mistake, one neither of us can afford. And I would ask you to believe me on this, even if you don't listen to anything else I say. Because it's important, Teale. I wouldn't have brought it up if it weren't."

Her throat was dry, and her heart was pounding slowly and steadily. Her face was warm where he touched it, and she couldn't seem to break away from his gaze. He was so close a mere breath would have closed the distance between them, yet the way he looked at her made him seem even closer than that. How easy it would be to say Yes, she believed him, Yes, she trusted him, Yes, she would do whatever he said. To lean forward and let her face rest against his chest, to feel his arms, warm and secure, encircle her, to lift her head and taste him and let her blood rush and senses open, to let him push everything else aside except what he could make her feel. And she wanted to. In that moment she wanted it more than anything else in the world.

She held his gaze. She took an unsteady breath. She said quietly, "I'm going to bust you, David Carey. I promise you that."

He smiled. His fingers moved slowly down from her forehead to the curve of her neck where they curled against her skin for just a moment in a brief gesture of affection. "No, darling," he answered gently. "You're not. I promise *you* that."

He dropped his hand and stepped away. Teale turned back to the cutting board and resumed her task with a hand that was somewhat less sure than before.

"So," David inquired as she began to assemble the ingredients in the bowl. "What did your partner think of our little rendezvous last night?"

"You mean what did he think of you?"

He shrugged. "That, too."

"What makes you think I'd even ask him?"

"I know about partners," he answered. "And you and Sam seem particularly close. I don't imagine there's much the two of you don't discuss."

Once again, his eerie ability to read her to the letter made her defensive instincts bristle. "As a matter of fact, Sam did have a few things to say." She began to spread mayonnaise on the bread. "Are you sure you want to hear?"

"I can take it."

"He thinks you're arrogant, phony and a little bit nauseating. He said he'd heard better lines at a singles bar and that you had the morals of an alleycat and absolutely no finesse. I believe he also mentioned the word 'sociopath.'"

David's eyes twinkled. "The typical response of a jealous male."

"Jealous? Of you?"

"Of you."

"Don't be ridiculous. Sam's my partner, nothing more."

"That's good to know," he smiled, and too late Teale realized the entire line of questioning had been directed at nothing more than finding out exactly what her relationship with Sam was. She knew she should have been annoyed, but in fact she was absurdly gratified.

"It's also good to know," he went on, "that you don't share Sam's, er, rather dubious opinion of me."

She put the sandwiches together and sliced them diagonally. "What makes you so sure I don't?"

"Oh, come on, Teale. Sociopath? No finesse?"

She pretended to consider the matter. "Well . . . I'll grant you finesse. To a certain extent, anyway."

"Thank you for that," he murmured. "I do try."

She handed him his plate and reached into the refrigerator for two cans of ginger ale. "Do you want a glass?"

He lifted an eyebrow. "Now who has no finesse?"

She thrust the cold can into his hand. "You're the one who wanted to go slumming tonight. Let's eat in the living room. The show's starting."

"And sociopath?" he persisted, as he followed her to the sofa. "You can't really believe that."

"What else would you call a man who makes a career out of preying on the weak and flaunting the laws of society?"

He flashed her a grin. "Smart?"

But this time Teale was not amused. Perhaps it was the peculiar intimacy of that moment in the kitchen, perhaps it was seeing him, as she had all night, in a new light. Perhaps it was nothing more than her emotions getting in the way of her professional judgment again. But she really wanted to know.

She sat on the sofa, arranging a coaster for her ginger ale, settling her plate in her lap. She looked at David as he sat beside her. "Why do you do it?" she asked seriously. "You're bright, articulate, well educated; you could do almost anything you wanted for a living. Why this?"

She half expected a flippant reply, or no reply at all. She was somewhat surprised when he answered, "I do it for the same reason you do, Teale." His tone was just as serious, just as matter-of-fact as hers had been. "There are dozens of other things you could do, just as there are for me. But none of them have quite the same appeal, do they? The glamour, the excitement, the danger, a new challenge every day. You and I are not ordinary people, and we would never be satisfied living ordinary lives. That's why."

She drew a breath to protest, resenting the comparison and wanting to deny it was true. But she couldn't. He was right. They were on opposite sides of the law, they were opposite personalities, they were poles apart in life-style and values, yet at the root of the matter there was something about them that was the same. They were equally matched in skill and determination, equally motivated to win, equitably trained for the job; they understood and yes, in some odd way, even respected each other. Warring generals sent out to destroy each other who, without the war, would have been best friends. There was something very unsettling in that realization.

Still, she felt as though she should make some token denial, but David forestalled her by clicking on the remote control. "Shh," he said intently. "The show's starting." And he settled back to watch.

Six

At some more rational point in her life Teale supposed she would look back on the evening she spent curled up on the sofa eating tuna fish and watching *Rear Window* with one of the most wanted criminals in the state as an aberration, a touch of eccentricity brought on by incipient job burnout or simple insanity. But at the time it was happening, nothing in the world could have seemed more natural—even though she did notice she spent more time watching David than she did the movie.

Five minutes into the show David took his glasses from his T-shirt pocket and put them on with a rather sheepish look. "All right," he admitted. "Driving, reading and close work. In fact, anything that requires I see more than three feet in front of my face."

"Aha," she teased him softly. "That explains why you kept saying I was beautiful—you never saw me!"

"No," he assured her. "That's why I stand so close to you—to make sure of what I'm seeing."

Teale had very little time for a social life, but she had never felt the paucity until now. Sitting with David, listening to the muted rumble of thunder far offshore, sipping ginger ale and doing nothing more complicated than watching an old movie on television . . . It was nice. It was difficult to remember that none of this was real, that they weren't just an ordinary man and woman enjoying a quiet evening at home. That, in fact, he represented everything she was trained to despise and she was the symbol of all he held in contempt. After a while, Teale stopped trying to remind herself. For the first time in what seemed like many years, she simply relaxed and enjoyed herself.

At some point in the evening—Teale didn't know how or when—she found David's arm around her shoulders and her head resting comfortably against his biceps. That, too, seemed only natural. She became aware of the warmth of his hand cupping her bare shoulder, the strength of the lean muscle beneath her head, the masculine scent of him, subtle, but unmistakably tantalizing. She noticed how soft the T-shirt material that stretched over his chest looked, and she wondered how it would feel to run her hands over that fabric, tracing the definition of the muscles underneath, feeling heat and firm flesh and the springy texture of hair. Wondering made her stomach tight, and she tried to reproach herself, but all she succeeded in doing was to make herself feel guilty.

She couldn't help it if she found him attractive, she tried to rationalize. She couldn't control her body's instinctive response to one of the sexiest men she'd ever met. That didn't mean she had to do anything about it. She was perfectly aware that the course of her thoughts was inappropriate, even dangerous, but that didn't stop her from fantasizing.

Damn it, David, she thought helplessly, *why did you have to be who you are?* Why did he have to be so bright and so amusing and so unceasingly fascinating? Why did he have to make her feel the way she did every time she looked at him? Why couldn't he be all those things and also be an ordinary man with an ordinary past and an ordinary job?

Why was it that for the first time in her life she had met a man who interested her on more than a surface level and he had to be a criminal?

Yet there was more to David Carey than just his criminal activities, and that was what puzzled—and frustrated—her most. His strange sense of honor, that disturbing streak of sincerity; his humor, his wit, his carefree savoir faire... his unnerving perception, his unshakable confidence, his unexpected gentleness. Even the way his eyes flashed when she had accused him of using her— *Damn.* How was she supposed to understand a man like that? And why was it suddenly so important to her that she try?

She glanced up at him, his face shadowed by the flickering screen, his expression intent upon the action before him, looking vulnerable and relaxed in his glasses and T-shirt. Not like a dangerous criminal. Like a sexy, attractive, oddly endearing man.

He's a game player, Captain Hollis said. Teale wanted to believe it was that simple, but she couldn't. As hard as she tried, she couldn't dismiss David Carey that easily.

"I love this part," David murmured. "Funny how it seems old hat now, but when it was first done..."

Firmly, she focused her attention back on the television set, and with no small effort on her part, soon was caught up in the suspense of the make-believe drama before her. But just as Jimmy Stewart heard the ominous footsteps outside his door, as he struggled to wheel his chair around the tiny apartment and frantically armed himself with flashbulbs, the lights flickered and went out.

"Oh, damn," said David, disappointed.

She couldn't help laughing. "I'll tell you how it comes out."

"It won't be the same."

Teale felt in the darkness for a candle on the skirted end table beside her. "There must be a storm somewhere up the line; it happens all the time. There are some matches in the drawer of that table next to you—can you reach them?"

She heard him fumbling around on the table, wincing as a muffled thud indicated the fate of one of her treasures. A stack of magazines went to the floor with a flutter of pages. "I can barely see in full daylight," David apologized. "In the dark . . ."

"Okay, stay still. I'll get them."

Rather than risk stumbling around the cluttered apartment in the dark, Teale stretched over him to reach the table. Perhaps that was a mistake.

She felt David's soft intake of breath as her breasts brushed his chest and her knee nudged his thigh. Searching for her balance, her hand pressed into his belt line and immediately jerked away; his hands lightly touched her bare waist to steady her. She assured herself the contact was unintentional and it was a silly, awkward moment. Nonetheless, there was a catch in her own breath when she felt his fingers on her unclothed skin, and she took perhaps a moment longer than she should fumbling in the drawer for the matches, wondering if his hands would tighten and turn her to him, and if in the dark their lips would seek each other's and meet, and if they did, what would happen next.

He slowly drew his hands away. She found the matches and straightened up, her breathing a little irregular and her hand somewhat unsteady as she struck a flame, but otherwise completely in control. "There," she said, as the candle wick caught and flared. "At least we can see what we're doing."

He smiled. "I liked it better when we couldn't."

Teale set the candle on the table before them. Its dim yellow glow illuminated an arc of about two feet from the center, leaving the rest of the room in soft shadows. Without the television and the air conditioner, the room was intensely silent, and she could hear the wind gently bending the trees outside. It's going to get stuffy in here before long, she thought, but she made no move to open the windows. She sat back on the sofa, her elbow resting on its back, her body turned toward David, and she looked at him.

"You look pretty in the candlelight," he said.

"Everyone looks pretty in candlelight," she answered.

And then, without forethought or conscious volition, she reached forward and slowly removed his glasses. He said nothing, nor did he move. She sat back on her heels, studying him. "Who are you, David Carey?" she asked softly.

In the uncertain candlelight there might have been a flicker of surprise in his eyes, a tightening of the facial muscles as though he were startled or unsure. But the expression, whatever it was, was gone in an instant, and his tone was casual and amused as he replied, "Who do you think I am?"

"I'm not sure," she answered earnestly. Her eyes remained fixed on his face, trying to resolve the dozen or more conflicting images she had gathered. "But I think I want to know."

He hesitated, but his expression was intent as his gaze moved over her face. "Is it really important to you?"

She nodded slowly.

A smile, vague and rather puzzled, gently traced the planes of his face. "All right," he agreed. "I'll tell you what I know.

"I was born in a little town north of San Diego— one of those undiscovered fishing villages that tourists like to stop and take snapshots of when they stumble on to it, and use words like 'quaint' and 'picturesque' to describe it. To me it was just home, and I had a great time growing up there. My dad owned a charter boat, and we used to go trolling at sunrise, and sometimes he'd take Mom and me out all day with his charter passengers. Once, I hooked a shark that was twice my size—I swear it. It took us four hours to land him, and you never saw a prouder kid than I was having my picture taken with that monster and posting it at the marina...." The smile lines at the corners of his eyes deepened with fond remembrance. "God, we had fun."

A shadow crossed his eyes, but his voice was deliberately casual as he went on. "Then Mom and Dad went out on the boat one day without me, a storm blew up, and they didn't come back. Of course I went through the usual trauma, but I think somewhere deep

inside I always knew that was the way they would have
wanted to go—on the sea, at the height of a storm, in
a blaze of glory.

"After that, my life changed. Uncle Raphe took me
in—he wasn't really my uncle of course, but an old
friend of the family." His brow drew together slightly,
as though reliving an old puzzlement. "I never knew
what favor it was my Dad did him that made him feel
he had to repay it in such a big way, and I guess I really
don't want to know. It doesn't matter, I suppose.
Those kinds of ties are thick, and Raphe was good to
me.

"I lived in the compound outside of San Francisco
with body guards, maids, three swimming pools—
every conceivable luxury. A rock star entertained at
my sixteenth birthday party. I had my own Maserati
before I was old enough to drive. I went to an exclu-
sive private school and was accepted by both Yale and
Harvard. But I had something more. I had a family. I
had discipline and love and good common-sense values and a man who was never too busy for me...a man
who took another man's son and made him his own."

He looked at her steadily, almost challengingly.
"This might sound naive, but it's the truth. I never
knew what kind of business Raphael Clealand was in
until he was indicted."

Teale almost held her breath, yearning to understand, hoping for the right answer...not even knowing what the right answer should be. "And when you
found out?"

His gaze didn't waver. "It didn't make any difference," he said simply. "I still loved him. How he made
his money didn't take away what he had done for me,

it didn't change the kind of man I knew him to be inside."

Then his lashes dropped, briefly obscuring his expression. "It made me angry," he admitted. "Not for the reasons you think, but because once I knew the truth I could see what it was costing him. The investigation, the pressures to hold it all together—it was killing him. Oh, I know the coroner's report said heart attack, but it was his business that killed him just as surely as if some rival kingpin's assassin had pulled the trigger. And that made me angry."

Teale released a slow, unsteady breath. "And so," she ventured softly, "you went into the business to more or less avenge your foster father's death."

For a moment he looked puzzled, as though he didn't know quite what she was talking about, then he smiled. "Yes, I suppose you could say that. In a small way. Not that what I do really has much effect on the overall scheme of things, but it makes me feel better to keep my hand in."

Teale nodded. She didn't know whether she felt better or worse for hearing this, but at least she understood. At least some part of it made sense to her.

She knew she should leave it alone, she knew that any effort she made would be futile, but she just couldn't help herself. She had to try, if for no other reason than to make it completely clear in her own mind. "And you really don't think you're doing anything wrong, do you?"

A soft laugh escaped him, and the mirth seemed completely inappropriate to the situation. "Do you mean do I ever question the rightness of my decision? Oh, yes, every day." And a note of soberness touched his tone as he met her eyes. "Even more, lately."

A small absurd hope flared within Teale, and he must have seen it in her eyes because he gave her no chance to pursue the subject.

"Now you know my history from birth to young adulthood," he said lightly, "and your police records will fill in the rest. If you want to know who I am, it's all there." He looked at her very intently, as though trying to telegraph some unspoken message she couldn't understand. "If you're willing to look hard enough."

And then he smiled, dismissing the moment. "Of course, that's true of everyone, I suppose. You, for instance. Now that I've bared my soul, I don't suppose you'd be willing to give me a hint or two about what makes Teale Saunders tick?"

She shrugged, in the same motion drawing her legs up to encircle them with her arms. David's eyes followed the motion; she hoped it didn't look defensive. "What you see is what you get. I have no secrets."

"What made you go into law enforcement?"

"Family tradition, I suppose. My father was a judge."

She didn't know what came over her then. Maybe it was the sense of anonymity the shadowed room afforded or the security of being safe inside while the wind rushed against the windows and whispered around the eaves. Perhaps it was the intimacy that had grown between them as David spoke or the way he waited in patient silence, as though understanding she had more to say. Perhaps it was simply knowing that with David Carey she could be honest because he, of all people, would never sit in judgment. Because he would understand.

She rested her chin on her knees. Without looking at David she began to speak, softly, almost as though to herself. "From the time I can remember, I idolized him. My mother died when I was six, and from that time he was the beginning and end of my world. In school, when we had to write a paper on our hero, other kids would write about Batman or Neil Armstrong—I'd write about my father. All day he'd sit on his throne dispensing justice with Solomonlike wisdom, but he never missed a school play or a PTA meeting, and I never would have gotten through high school if he hadn't spent three hours a night helping me with my algebra. We were close," she said, and her throat tightened up a little. "Really close."

She cleared her throat and went on. "There was never any choice about my going into law. It was all I heard about from the day I was old enough to understand—the symmetry of it, the grandness of it and, yes, even the fallibility of it. The magnificence of an institution designed to govern such a large body of people for generations and generations to come. I was hooked at a very young age. My father always expected me to become a lawyer, and I guess I did, too, for a while. But at some point I guess I realized I didn't really want to compete with my father in his own arena, or maybe I was afraid I wouldn't be able to live up to his standards—or my own. Anyway, I wasn't cut out for a cerebral life. I liked the action of police work, the excitement, and—" her lips turned down a little, wryly, as she remembered David's previous words "—the danger, I suppose."

Her smiled faded as the memories came back. If David had interrupted her then with a question or a comment, she wouldn't have gone on. She hadn't expected it to be this hard. She had never told anyone this before, and she didn't know why she was speaking of it now. She wished she had never begun the story.

But David simply sat there, listening and waiting, and she had no choice but to go on. She suddenly realized that she wanted to continue. She needed to say this, to repeat the words and relive the tragedy, to face it at last. And David Carey had given her the opportunity to do so.

"Four years ago," she began steadily, "there was a scandal. My father was accused of taking bribes. He denied it, of course, but it looked like an airtight case. I was so—horrified and humiliated. All those years, worshiping him, believing he was the incarnation of Justice itself, believing all those things he said about honesty and fairness and our duty to the integrity of the democratic system. I had built my whole life on him and his values only to find out that he had been lying all along and that the one thing—the one person in my life—I had never had cause to doubt was as corrupt and as flawed as the streets of the city I was trying to clean up. Here I was, a police officer with an impeccable record, up for promotion, and my father was the object of a grand-jury investigation and one of the biggest scandals to hit the city in years. Looking back," she said bitterly, "I don't know whether I was more upset about the scandal or my own embarrassment."

Even as she spoke the anger came back, the choking sense of hurt and betrayal—the guilt. There was no stopping it now. The words came rushing out, memory on top of memory, pain redoubled with the telling. "I wanted to believe him. But I was an officer of the *law*. I knew about facts and evidence and what was written in black and white. There was a part of me that knew my father could never be guilty of such a thing, but I had sworn to uphold the law, I was trained to look at nothing more than the evidence and...I guess I hadn't learned yet that sometimes an officer's most important tool is his own instinct.''

She felt wetness on her cheeks, hot and salty, and her throat was thick. But she couldn't stop. ''And even though...I tried to believe him, I guess he must have seen in my eyes that I didn't...Because I will never forget the way he looked before he went out that day...'' Her voice caught and choked, and then became very calm.

''No one else would do it,'' she said, ''so he set out to prove his own innocence. And he was killed by the men who had tried to set him up. It all came out later. He was innocent, but he had to die to prove it. No one would believe him. Not even his own daughter.''

The tears fell, scalding, silent and bitter. She didn't fight them. And when David gently drew her into his arms, she let him; she wound her fingers into the fabric of his T-shirt and let the tears fall while he held her, and it felt good. The guilt was still there, the anger and the helplessness, but the shame was not so great anymore. She had told someone. She had told David.

He said nothing, and she was grateful for that. He didn't offer meaningless platitudes or expressions of sympathy; he made no attempt to conjure up expiation. What he gave her was quiet understanding and acceptance. And that was all she needed.

At length the tears expended themselves, and she lay against him, exhausted by emotion yet strangely purged, peaceful for the first time in many years. She could hear the slow strong beating of his heart, feel the dampness of his shirt beneath her fevered face, and she thought distantly, there is something right about this. Something so...good. And she felt as though she could stay that way forever.

"I never told anyone that before," she said softly.

She felt something brush against her hair—his fingertips, perhaps, or his lips. "I'm glad you told me."

She took a breath, trying to strengthen herself for the moment when she must inevitably move away, and released it shakily. "When I came here, I felt so ashamed and guilty. I didn't even tell anyone who my father was. The story was in all the papers, and I didn't want anyone to know. I kept thinking if I had done my job better, if I had worked harder to find the real criminals—if I had *believed* him..."

Unexpectedly, the tears welled up again, but this time she scrubbed them away angrily. "Damn," she whispered, and made herself move away from David and the comfort he offered. She sat up straight, made one last swipe at her face and drew another deep breath. In a moment, she was in control.

"So." She looked at him, apologizing for neither the confession nor the tears. "Now you know who I am," she said simply, "and why I'm the way I am. Why what I do is more than just a job and why I have to be so absolutely certain I always do it right. I guess—" And she hesitated there, uncertain, hovering on the edge of a discovery she wasn't entirely sure she wanted to make. "We're both atoning for something in a way, aren't we?"

He looked at her soberly. "Yes. I think we are."

But that was too much. Too many feelings, too many recognitions, too many changes; perhaps too many truths. In these past few minutes she had been closer to David Carey than she had been to any other person in her life, and nothing between them could possibly ever be the same again. And how was she supposed to deal with that?

At the moment she couldn't deal with it at all. She stood abruptly. "It's warm in here, isn't it?"

She crossed the room to the patio door that opened out onto a wide courtyard. She slid it open and stepped outside.

There was a crisp, electric feeling to the air. The wind bent the tops of trees overhead but only occasionally did a cool gust dip down to touch Teale's skin. The buildings surrounding her were dark, and the sky overhead was layered in pillows of gray-black that were occasionally backlit by a silent flash of lightning. The night was charged and static, poised on the edge of excitement.

Teale stood there, breathing deeply, tasting the night and letting the rush of the wind cleanse her mind. She had learned to love coastal storms since she had been here, even the distant, unfulfilled ones like this. Her nervous system responded on an instinctive level to the changes in the air, making her feel invigorated and renewed . . . eager.

The flashes of heat lightning, the buffeting currents of wind, the swelling cloud cover were potent and alive; they reflected the changes that were taking place within her. There was the taste of danger in the air, just as there was an edge of danger to her changing relationship with David, but she didn't feel threatened. She let herself be carried along on the tides of change; she almost welcomed it.

She heard his footsteps behind her, but he didn't speak for a time. They stood together, watching the distant storm, and in their silence they were as close as two people could be.

He said softly, after a time, "It's magnificent, isn't it?"

"Yes." She rubbed her fingers over the gooseflesh on her arms, and, noticing, he slipped his arm around her, warming her.

"No rain," she commented unnecessarily.

"We won't get any out of this one," he responded with the sagacity of a longtime sea dweller. "Just a lot of wind and thunder."

"I like it better this way. Before the rain. It's—powerful, somehow."

"Expectation always is."

She glanced at him, her heart speeding a little. His face was quiet and sternly etched in the darkness, absorbed in the beauty of the storm. Where their bodies touched—from shoulder to hip—and where his arm lightly encircled her, she was warm; the remainder of her body was cool in comparison. Expectation was what she felt as she stood with him in the dark and the wind; it soared through her veins like a potion and tightened the muscles of her stomach.

He looked down at her gently, referring to their previous conversation as though there had never been an interruption. "Is that all you are, Teale? An officer of the law, a woman with a job to do?"

She had to move her eyes away. The rhythm of her heart was a slow uneven pumping, and her throat was dry. "I'm good at my job."

"So am I. But lately...I've come to realize that's not enough. There has to be more to life, I think."

She could feel a tightening in her chest, spreading upward to her throat. The muscles in her arms and legs strained, and every nerve in her body pulsed with awareness. She wanted to be held by him; she wanted to hold him, fiercely, with all the strength of her body. She made herself stand still.

"Do you mean—like significant others?" She tried to keep her voice light.

"Yes," he admitted slowly. "But until tonight, I don't think I ever realized how important that was."

Her heart skipped then resumed its beat. *No*, she thought firmly. *I'm not going to let this happen.* It was only the aftermath of traumatic memories, the expenditure of emotion, the wild, provocative character of the night. She was vulnerable, she was confused. She wasn't going to let this happen.

She said steadily, "I prefer to concentrate on my job. It's not easy for me to share myself with other people."

He said gently, "I know."

Then she had to look at him. In his gaze was written a quiet understanding of the truth; it was the same thing that was in her own. She had shared herself with him. It didn't matter how or why, whether it was wrong or right. There was a bond between them now; there was no breaking it or ignoring it. And for just that moment, as the hot electric wind swept down to buffet her and David's gaze held her like an embrace, it didn't matter who he was at all.

She slowly lifted her arms to encircle him; he bent toward her. They kissed.

Passion flared, swift and intense. The gentle, exploratory nature of last night's first kiss was gone, and they came together in mutual urgency, greedy and sure. His power swept through her, charging and galvanizing her. She drank of him hungrily; her fingers pressing and shaping the straining muscles of his back, exploring the damp warm texture of his neck beneath his hair, traveling down to his waist and tracing his shape. She felt his hands upon her naked back, pressing into her ribs, the length of his strong hard thighs and the hardness of his pelvis against hers. Exhilaration flooded her, and a sweet wild madness blotted out everything else but David and her need for him.

His lips left hers, but only for a moment, to whisper her name, to brush her face, to touch the sensitive hollow just beneath her ear. A thrill of desire went through her and left her weak. His face was a blur before her, a textured collage of softness and roughness, fever and dampness, beneath her shaky fingertips.

His hand traveled slowly up her ribs and slipped beneath her halter, cupping her breast. She lost her breath, and her muscles went watery as his fingers lightly caressed her hard, swollen nipple. A knot of need tightened low in her belly and spread on quivering wires of sensation to every part of her body. Unconsciously, she pressed herself against him, aching for him, wanting him blindly.

He lowered his head, he kissed both of her breasts, one after the other, deeply, lingering, through the material. The ache had become painful, and she moaned with it.

"Teale," he whispered, holding her. She could hear his breathing and feel it against her neck. The thunder of his heartbeat matched her own. "Let's go inside. Let me love you."

Yes, she thought, and closed her eyes. *Yes....*

But, against his shoulder, she was shaking her head, slowly and deliberately. "No," she whispered hoarsely.

She brought her hands to his arms, tightened them there, and then pushed herself away. He didn't try to stop her.

She was shaking, heated and weak. Every nerve in her body stung and ached, crying out in protest against the sudden deprivation. She wanted him. Nothing was going to change that. The ache wouldn't go away. But even as she knew that, she said again, "No."

She saw his face, flushed and passion-hazed, and his eyes, light and dark. The wind swept down again and tossed his hair, except for a single strand that was caught in the dampness of his forehead. She wanted to touch that strand and smooth it away; she wanted simply to touch him, one more time. With all the will in her being, she did not.

She caught her lower lip between her teeth and tried to stop the trembling. She looked at him helplessly, wanting him to understand, knowing that he already did.

She said as steadily as she could, "If we—made love tonight, could you be sure it wasn't just because—I was doing my job?"

He answered hoarsely, but without hesitation. "Yes."

An ache swelled inside her throat that felt like the beginning of tears. She had to turn away, and she shook her head sadly. "I couldn't," she whispered.

After a moment, he came up behind her and lightly dropped his hand onto her shoulder. Nothing more, just that gentle, comforting touch of his hand. Then she heard the breath of his sigh. "Oh, Teale," he said heavily, "this isn't good, is it?"

Her eyes blurred hotly; determinedly she blinked them clear. She couldn't find her voice, so she simply shook her head, violently.

In a moment, with a light pressure on her shoulder, he turned her to face him. He tried to smile, but there was a seriousness and a hunger in his eyes she couldn't ignore. "We're playing by a whole new set of rules now, aren't we?" he asked gently.

"Yes," she whispered, because there was no point in denying it.

He nodded. His gaze moved over her face once, briefly, and then back to her eyes. Again, he tried to smile. "Well, that's what makes life interesting, isn't it? You never know the outcome."

Perhaps. But she knew what would become of David and her: nothing. Nothing at all. It simply wasn't possible.

She straightened her shoulders and lifted her chin. The next words were among the most difficult she had ever had to say. "Some things haven't changed, David. The most important things. It would be dangerous for you to forget that."

He dropped his gaze briefly. "I won't."

When he looked at her again his expression had altered, almost by force of will, becoming casual and light. "Do you need a ride to work tomorrow?" he asked.

She shook her head quickly, adamantly. To show up for work in David's sports car, to have everyone in the department speculating and grinning and nudging themselves, to risk having the captain take her off the case.... "I'll call Sam."

"All right, then." His eyes lingered on hers for a moment longer. "I'll see you soon."

She nodded.

He moved forward and kissed her lightly on the forehead. "Good night, Teale."

He turned and walked back into the apartment, guided by the light of the candle through the living room and toward the front door. But Teale stayed outside long after she'd heard the door close, watching the distant storm, alone with her own troubled thoughts.

David spent a long time driving along the coast road because he didn't want to go back to his house while people were still there. He parked for a time and watched the lightning illuminate the clouds, forming ominous shapes in fleeting revelations. He was accustomed to dealing with crises; the unexpected was routine for him. But he had never had to face a crisis like this, and the usual formulas he employed to solve complex problems seemed pat and didn't apply. Perhaps it was because, for the first time in many years, he was being forced to listen to his heart and not his head.

"Imagine," he murmured to himself at last, with a weary, slightly amused shake of his head. "At my age...."

The party was over when he got home, but George was waiting up for him.

"How did it go?" David asked without interest. The power, he noticed, was on at his house. He wondered if it had been restored at Teale's.

"The usual. There was a message." George watched David alertly as he handed him a folded note. "Diangelo. He's made the first move."

David read the message without expression, then crumpled it into an ashtray. He sat down heavily, swinging his feet up onto the coffee table, his arms folded across his chest. His eyes were brooding and abstract, and he asked abruptly after a moment, "Do you ever think about dumping it all? Just sailing away to some island in the South Pacific and leaving it all behind?"

George snorted. "Only every day and twice on Sundays." He touched a match to the paper in the ashtray and watched as tendrils of smoke began to curl upward.

"I've been thinking about it a lot lately."

George looked at him, and then his expression sharpened into amazement. "You're serious."

David said nothing.

George shook his head in a mixture of astonishment and derision. "Man, you're crazy. You couldn't get out even if you wanted to. And you don't want to. You've got too much invested—we've all got too much invested. You'd be climbing the walls inside a month."

"Maybe," David agreed absently. "But sometimes I think . . . well, this just might be my last job."

George stared at him, and suddenly his eyes narrowed in understanding. "It's that woman," he pronounced decisively. "That female cop. She's getting to you!"

David didn't respond at once. His brow remained drawn in heavy, contemplative silence; his hands laced over his chest. Then he stood slowly, and his smile was sad. "That she is," he admitted, and turned toward the bedroom. "That she surely is."

Seven

During the next week a tropical depression hovered off the coast, unwilling to upgrade itself to a full-size storm, gathering energy, waiting. The sky remained swollen and overcast, and the humidity was so high that Teale's hair was damp by midmorning. Occasional afternoon thunderstorms would erupt, promising an end to the heat and the tension, but in fact would do no more than spatter the ground with a few fat drops of rain before retreating again, gathering force for the grand event everyone knew was coming.

For 235 dollars Teale retrieved her car and her freedom of movement. She lost the argument with Captain Hollis over wearing a wire when she was with David. She said nothing to Sam or the captain about the evening spent with David in her apartment watching *Rear Window* and listening to the distant storm.

The course of the Carey investigation was just as
static and oppressive as the atmosphere outside. Every
move Teale made was hampered by yards of red tape,
every avenue she opened turned out to be a blind alley, forcing her at last to declare bitterly that it was no
wonder David Carey was always a step ahead of the
game—he didn't have to deal with the bureaucracy.

After more effort than should reasonably have been
required, Teale finally got a look at the Diangelo file.
She studied the photograph of a short, balding mid-
dle-aged man—someone's grandfather or favorite
uncle. She tried to imagine the malevolence behind
that bland countenance, and when she read his record
she didn't have to imagine. It made her ill. How could
David be involved with a man like that?

Stay away from him, David had told her. *He's bad
news, Teale, and you're about to get in over your head*.

"Still working on your straight-line theory?" Sam
commented over her shoulder. There was a touch of
disgust in his voice. He, too, was frustrated with the
course of the investigation and was anxious to move
on to something more promising. "Honey, the only
way you're going to get close enough to Diangelo to
recognize him from that photograph is if David Carey
introduces you to him at a dinner party. And the way
things are going, that doesn't look very likely, does
it?"

"It doesn't hurt to cover all the angles," she replied somewhat shortly, and closed the file. "We're
sure not getting anywhere taking the long way
around."

She opened David's file and began to go through it
again, slowly, page by page.

Sam groaned. "What the hell do you think you're going to get from that? You've read it so often the print's beginning to fade. Besides, there's nothing in there lover boy hasn't already told you in all its gory detail."

"Yes, there is," she said slowly. She tapped her pencil against the pages thoughtfully. "Something's not right here."

"Yeah, well, I'll tell you what's not right. This whole investigation, that's what. We're sitting here spinning our wheels while every night David Carey is raking in hundreds of thousands of illegal dollars. I'll tell you the truth, Saunders, I'm about ready to recommend we wrap the whole thing. Bust Carey, be satisfied with what we've got and hope for a better shot at Diangelo next time around."

"No," she said, perhaps too quickly. "You know we can't do that. Besides," she added, somewhat more casually, "I already tried it with Hollis and it didn't fly."

Not giving him a chance to question her for details, she pointed to a page of the file. "Look at this. These five years he was in Europe—but Interpol has nothing on him."

Sam was unimpressed. "So? Our records exchange with foreign agencies isn't exactly infallible, you know. Hell, we have enough trouble keeping up with information between states."

"Exactly." Teale thumped the page again. "Here, between Florida and Connecticut—another year is missing. And two years beginning in '84."

"Come on, Teale, the man's a shrewd operator. Do you think he's going to let us keep records of every heist he pulls? Men like Carey don't get caught, that's all."

"That's just what I mean. This record is spotty. If he was as good as we think he is, we should have nothing. Instead we have sporadic indication of meaningless connections and petty charges...just enough to let us know he's dirty but not enough to tell us *how* dirty. And nothing whatsoever that links anything together. Damn," she sighed. "I'd sure like to know what went on in these blank spaces."

Sam hesitated. "Well," he said, "I've got a friend in Central Records at the capitol. You want me to give her a call?"

Teale lifted an eyebrow. "Her?"

He grinned. "All my best friends are women."

"Maybe you'd like to run up there and check into it personally."

He considered that. "Maybe I would. As I recall, she makes a hell of a chicken-fried steak."

"Call her," Teale advised. "Make her set those computer wheels to work. There's got to be *something* more on Carey than we have here."

Teale breathed a sigh of relief when he was gone. At least he had something to keep him busy. As for Teale, she didn't know what she expected from Central Records, or even why she wanted it. Was she really looking for something to help her break this case—or was she hoping for something that would prove David's innocence?

During the day, she did her job, she devoted herself to the routine of investigation, she assured herself there was no conflict of interest. She did not forget what David Carey was: an underworld figure, an illegal operator, a collection of facts on paper. Not a

threat to the safety of the free world, certainly; not a
mass murderer or a war criminal or a terrorist, but an
enemy to the way of law and order and a key figure in
a criminal investigation. And Teale pursued the investigation with just the amount of vigor it deserved,
no more and no less.

But at night ... at night everything was different.

She saw David Carey almost every evening, always
wearing a hidden wire, always with Sam somewhere
close in attendance. In the morning she would duti-
fully turn in the tapes and stoically receive Sam's
comments. "Now I know why I never asked you out,"
he would grumble in passing. Or, "Real fun evening,
Saunders. I only fell asleep twice." Or, "Next time
pick a movie I haven't seen, okay?" And finally,
"What are you doing with that guy, anyway—playing
pinochle? I could get more information out of a
stopped clock—not to mention more entertainment."

What Sam did not see were the looks that passed
between she and David across a candlelit dinner table, the accidental brushings of hands that lingered or
the simple smiles. David said nothing because he knew
about the wire, of course, and the things he might have
liked to say were for her ears only. Teale, recognizing
that, was deeply touched. He expertly fielded the
questions she felt compelled to ask, relevant to the investigation, and she was relieved when he did so.

For there were other rewards. When they were together they acted like ordinary people, real people,
people who were getting to know each other and enjoyed every moment of it. They went to movies and
had lively discussions about them afterward. Over
dinner they talked about books and music and nou-
velle cuisine. It bored Sam, but it fascinated Teale.

They went to a seashore carnival, and she discovered
David had a weakness for cotton candy and that he
loved the roller coaster as much as she did. There was
no pressure, no deceit, no sidestepping emotional
dangers. They were simply at ease with each other, and
Teale treasured every moment of it. The constraints of
her job—and the hidden microphone—both pro-
tected and freed her.

And Sam didn't know about the notes. Over dinner, at the movies, walking along the beach, David
would pull out scraps of paper or pick up cocktail
napkins and scribble, "Your eyes are so bright I can
see myself in them. Does that mean you're happy?"
or "I want to kiss you so badly I ache." Or, occasionally, "This one's for Sam." Whereupon he would
launch into a tale of his supposed exploits that was so
horrific, so outrageous and absurd, that there could
be no doubt it was taken directly from a Mario Puzo
novel, leaving Teale in convulsions of laughter and
causing Sam to comment dourly the next morning,
"The man's a maniac."

Sometimes, late at night, as she lay in bed alone,
Teale wondered how much longer she could possibly
keep up this double life. How much longer could she
go on compartmentalizing her thoughts and her emotions—Teale the cop for daytime, Teale the woman for
night—when David Carey was the pivot on which all
compartments revolved? She told herself she was only
following orders; she was keeping an eye on David, she
was building his trust, and if anything began to break
in the operation she would be in a position to be the
first to know. But inside she knew it was much, much
more than that. Because when she made out her re-
ports every morning she did not include the looks, the

smiles, the notes. She did not include the way she felt every time she was with him, and those feelings were not going to go away.

She avoided thinking about the time when she would be forced to take action on the investigation. That inevitable moment when all the pieces fell into place and there was no more need for candlelight dinners and walks on the beach and quiet conversation. That time when the evidence was collected and the warrant was issued and she would have to pull out her badge and say to David, "You're under arrest." She knew it was coming. But she couldn't think about it.

She couldn't think about that night when they stood on her patio and watched the storm, she couldn't think about the way his eyes lit up when he smiled or the way her stomach tightened when he looked at her or how good it felt to laugh with him or how much she wanted to touch him, sometimes. She couldn't think about her feelings at all, because she knew if ever she allowed the contents of one compartment to spill over into the other she wouldn't be able to deal with any of it. She didn't dare examine anything that was happening too closely; she convinced herself that her integrity was intact by simply not questioning it.

And then the evening came when she couldn't avoid the truth any longer.

She and David were having iced capuccino at one of the trendy new sidewalk cafés on the boardwalk. It was sunset, and the thick gray sky was laced with scallops of bright red and orange. The sea was murky and still. At the horizon a cloud dipped down and sprayed the water with a foggy curtain of rain, and Teale was fascinated by the effect.

"I wish I could paint," she murmured. "I would like to frame that and hang it in my living room."

"There's not even room to hang a hat in your living room," he teased her. "Much less a painting." But his eyes followed her gaze over the rumpled beach and past the last few swimmers to the horizon. "I had an oil painting once, of rain at sea. It didn't entirely capture the true effect, but close enough."

"What happened to it?"

He shrugged. "I never keep anything for long. One of the hazards of my profession."

And so it went, idle conversation about nothing of consequence, just easy talk between people who were almost friends. He passed her a folded cocktail napkin, and Teale opened it, anticipating his message as she always did, expecting some amusing remark about Sam or some flattering or tender comment that would make her blush.

The note read, "I think I'm falling in love with you."

Teale's heart jumped and stopped, and then beat so fast it seemed to fill her entire chest. She stared at the words. Something swelled and soared within her—it might have been happiness or it might have been terror. *I think I'm falling in love with you....*

She raised her eyes slowly to David, but his expression had not changed. His eyes were still studying the horizon, his profile strong and clear. Then he moved his eyes to her, and the tenderness she saw there, the quiet and certain truth, closed around her heart until it hurt.

Then he said easily, "Are you ready to go?"

Teale's hand closed around the napkin, and she nodded wordlessly.

There were no more notes that night. He walked her to her door as he always did; he did not kiss her goodnight, as he never did. Teale went inside and turned on all the lights, and she listened until the sound of David's footsteps had disappeared. She opened the crumpled cocktail napkin and looked at the words scrawled there for a very long time.

And then she began to cry.

All right, Teale, she told herself as she went into work the next morning. You're a grown woman. More than that, you're a professional. This has gone too far. You know what you have to do.

She hadn't slept at all the night before, and she knew it showed on her face. Her skin was bloodless, and her eyes were circled with mauve; the humidity was so oppressive that even her clothes felt weighted down by it. She didn't care; she hardly even noticed. The important thing was that she had come to a decision.

She must ask to be removed from the case.

What would happen after that, she didn't know. Somehow she had to come to terms with what she could no longer deny were her feelings for David Carey. Somehow she had to convince herself that all her training, all her study and work and devotion to the law had not been simply window dressing to be tossed aside for the first handsome man who offered her a life of crime. She had to find a way to reaffirm that she was who she thought she was: a woman with unbreachable standards and principles who knew her purpose in life and had the courage to follow it.

She needed time; she needed distance. She needed never to see David Carey again. She needed to see David more than anything in the world.

Sam was waiting for her as she came into the office. "You look like hell," he greeted her.

"Shocking, isn't it? Is Hollis in?"

"Yeah, but listen." The peculiar frown on Sam's face made her hesitate and come over to his desk. "You remember that friend of mine in Central Records?"

"The one with the chicken-fried steak?"

"Also the one with the computers. The woman is a whiz. You want it; she's got it. There's nothing she can't get her hands on—except David Carey's personal history."

Teale stared at him, not quite understanding.

Sam leaned back in his chair. "It's been lifted, babe," he elaborated, "right out of the tape banks. What we've got on Carey is all there is. Anywhere. In the world. Period."

Teale frowned. "Oh, come on. There's got to be something. Income-tax records, passport applications, driver's licenses, service record, credit cards for heavens' sake—"

"Exactly the kind of paper trail somebody went to a hell of a lot of trouble to eliminate."

Teale shook her head slowly. "It doesn't make any sense."

"It does to somebody who doesn't want to be traced."

"That's ridiculous. A man who's trying to create a new identity does it with full backup, all the way back to the birth certificate. He doesn't leave blank spaces for people to find."

"Maybe he does if he changes identity so often he doesn't have *time* to fill in the blanks. Or maybe—" he looked at her soberly "—he's so well-protected he doesn't have to worry about the cops finding out what he's up to."

The prickle of a shiver went down Teale's spine. "Who would have that kind of power?"

"Diangelo," Sam replied without hesitation. "The evidence seems to indicate, my dear, that somebody has invested a lot in our boy. My guess is he goes back a lot further with the Organization than this one job— and that he's placed a lot higher up in it than we ever guessed."

Teale didn't make it to Captain Hollis's office that day. She went to her desk and spent a great deal of time shuffling papers and looking busy, all the while trying to assimilate this new information, to understand it or excuse it.

Of course they had always known there was a connection with Diangelo. But this *kind* of connection? Even a man as powerful as Diangelo wouldn't take this kind of risk for a minor-league operator. It was expensive, it was dangerous, and no one would go to that kind of trouble unless he expected a big payoff. And that kind of payoff was not forthcoming from the small-time gambling house David Carey was running on the beach.

Then what was really going on in that house? And who *was* David Carey?

Of course there were other explanations for a spotty file and the inaccessibility of his records. Maybe he was sloppy. Maybe he didn't expect anyone to look hard enough to find the blank spaces. Maybe he didn't know about or have access to the kind of sophisticated techniques it would take to completely cover his tracks. Maybe it was all a mistake.

Those were all perfectly reasonable, plausible explanations. Then why did she have to think the worst?

Because she was a law officer, that was why. Because, contrary to anything suggested otherwise by the Constitution or any other document, she was trained to believe in guilt until innocence was proven. To do otherwise in her line of work would not only be naive but dangerous. And because, for the sake of her peace of mind, she simply had to know the truth.

At three o'clock, David called.

"I had to call five times before you answered the phone," he said. "I was running out of ways to disguise my voice."

Her heart began a heavy, dry thumping. She said, "Yes, this is Detective Saunders."

"Good girl," he said in soft approval. "This isn't an official call. I need to see you this afternoon, alone."

She picked up a pencil and pretended to write something down. "Okay. Good."

"Can you meet me by the pier, about five? I think we need to talk," he added quietly.

Teale kept her voice casually polite. "Sounds great. I'll pick it up on my way home from work. Thanks."

She hung up the telephone and glanced across at Sam's desk. "Television set," she explained to his inquiring look. "Can you believe it took them two weeks to replace a wire on the circuit board?"

Sam shrugged and turned back to his paperwork. "That's the American way."

So now she had done it. She had lied to her partner, she had declined to report contact from a suspect, and she had agreed to a secret meeting with a person under investigation without informing her superior. Were there any more rules she could break? What was happening to her?

Her palms were damp with guilt, and she hated herself, but when she left the office she still hadn't spoken to Captain Hollis, and she wasn't wearing a wire.

David was waiting for her in the parking lot next to the pier. He was wearing shorts and a collarless shirt of soft cotton weave, his hair was sunburnished and shiny, and the smile of greeting in his eyes made the muggy gray day seem bright and fresh. Teale felt frumpy and worn in her rumpled skirt and blouse, with her wilted hair and circled eyes. But David seemed not to notice. Before she could say a word, he stepped forward and took her arms, and in full view of anyone who wanted to see, he kissed her on the lips.

"I've been wanting to do that all week," he said softly. "I don't think I could have waited another minute."

Teale's lips still tingled with the soft surprise of his kiss, and her blood pumped with instinctive anticipation of more. The light in his eyes washed through her like a slow, cleansing wave, and the dark disturbing thoughts of the day, even the torment of the night, seemed very far away.

She smiled. "Is that why you wanted me to meet you?"

"Partly," he admitted. "Maybe the biggest part. But there's something else." He took her hand and pulled her toward his car. "Let's go for a drive. I want to show you something."

He seemed so eager and excited—almost boyish—
that she couldn't help laughing. "I thought you'd
given up kidnapping."

"I don't remember too many complaints about the
last time."

"That was because I have a weakness for lobster."

"This is even better."

"Shrimp Creole?"

"Just wait and see."

It wasn't until they were speeding along the coastal
highway that the euphoria of seeing him again began
to fade, and Teale thought wonderingly, What power
he has over me. Eight hours ago she had been ready to
ask for a transfer because of him; since then she had
learned alarming, incriminating things about him,
dark suspicions had been stirred up, and she had come
here intending to confront him with them. But all he
had to do was look at her and she was no longer
thinking like a police officer. In his presence she was
simply Teale the woman with all her weaknesses and
all her foibles and, at the moment, feeling very weak
and confused inside.

And that was more than half the reason she had
come to him today. Because last night he had written
I think I'm falling in love with you, and at that moment she had known she could no longer keep Teale
the woman and Teale the detective in separate compartments. Her two worlds had collided, and she knew
she couldn't go on like this any longer.

She said, "I lied to my partner for you."

David reached across the console and took her
hand, squeezing it gently. "I'm sorry you had to do
that."

He sounded as though he meant it, and that made it much more difficult to go on. She looked down at their hands, twined together, light and dark, large and small. A study in opposites.

"I almost asked to be transferred from the case today," she said quietly.

His hand squeezed hers lightly, in comfort and reassurance. "I know it's hard for you, Teale. It won't be much longer, I promise."

She looked up at him intently. His bronze profile, muted in the light of the overcast day, his hair curling gracefully around his ear, his expression quiet and relaxed and...innocent. *David, don't do this to me*, she thought suddenly, fiercely. *Please don't let this be happening....*

But her voice was very calm as she asked, "How do you know that, David?"

He glanced at her and smiled. It was a gentle smile, almost reproving, and it said, Don't ask.

Out loud he said, "You haven't asked where we're going."

Teale looked around at the bleak, still day, the disappearing asphalt, the ragged seascape speeding by. She closed her eyes and leaned her head back against the headrest. "To the ends of the earth, I hope," she sighed tiredly.

David's hand tightened on hers, affectionately, once more, and they didn't speak again for the rest of the trip.

Teale didn't notice how far they'd gone until she opened her eyes to a vastly changed landscape. The marshes swept away on either side of them, dark gray-green, flat, vast and surrealistically still for as far as the eye could see. It was a stunning sight, potent and throbbing with life, yet as perfect as an oil painting.

Even the air had taken on a different color and texture, slightly greenish in cast and grainy with the power of an impending storm. The sky had dropped so low one could almost walk into it, spinning out tunnels of clouds that dripped over the marsh like pointing fingers ready to strike. Everything was uncannily silent, poised on the edge of expectancy. In such a place Teale wanted to hold her breath for fear of disturbing the delicate balance of beauty.

David stopped the car, and they got out. "My God," Teale said softly. "It's incredible."

The air had a funny taste to it, salty and stale, yet rich with the verdancy of growing things. Nothing moved, not even a breeze, but the soaking humidity was gone and the air seemed cooler. Teale recognized the faint electric scent of an impending storm.

David gestured to a cedar house suspended on stilts at the edge of the marsh, and, taking her arm, guided her toward it. "The ocean breaks away on the back side of the house," he said. His voice sounded muted in the heavy stillness. "The view is unobstructed for miles."

There was an unreality about it all, a sense of disorientation. Walking through the strange yellow light, looking at the three dimensional cloud formations that hung over the marsh, was like moving through a dream. Not even their footsteps echoed. It was beautiful, all absorbing and oddly alarming.

They mounted the steps to the house, and David took out a key.

"What are you doing?" Teale demanded. "Whose house is this?"

"No one's, yet." He opened the door and gestured her inside. "Come in, look around."

Teale hesitated, looking back over the marsh. "David, there's a storm coming. I don't think—"

"I know there's a storm coming, and if we don't hurry we're going to be stuck in it. Go on in."

Teale stepped inside. It was dark and musty-smelling, the way vacation homes often are when they haven't been used for a time. "Is this what you wanted me to see?" she asked, puzzled.

"That's right."

David closed the door and pressed the light switch. Two lamps blotted out the eerie quality of the faint daylight and painted the room in warm, cozy colors. It was a pleasant house with many windows and driftwood paneled walls. There was a sunken living room and a large fireplace in gray stone, and from the sliding glass doors that opened off the dining area Teale could see the dark choppy waters of the Atlantic. A view of the marsh swept away on two sides.

"It's nice," she said hesitantly. It *was* nice, only she didn't understand why he had brought her here.

"It has three bedrooms, two baths and a fully equipped kitchen. The master bath has a Jacuzzi. I'm thinking of buying it."

Teale, absently running her hand over an end table, looked up at him. "You have a house."

His expression was patient and tinged with amusement. "You know I don't own that house."

"Who does? Diangelo?"

She hadn't meant to bring it up like that, so abruptly, so much like an interrogating officer. But once it was done, she was glad.

A measure of surprise touched his eyes, and then absolute opaqueness. "As a matter of fact," he responded casually, "I don't know who owns it. I lease it from a real-estate company. Of course," he went on, walking over to the sunflower-print sofa and examining it critically, "I'd want to redecorate. It might even be fun. Do you know, I'm thirty-five years old and I've never decorated my own place? I'm not even sure what my taste is."

Distant thunder rolled, muted but powerful. Teale had a sudden impression of how isolated they were, and how alone. No electronic wire connected her to Sam and the real world this time, no city lights, no familiar surroundings. No one knew where she was, and there would be no excuses or explanations to make in the morning. There was nothing to come between her and her own feelings, and nothing to protect her from David . . . or her own desires.

Abruptly, she walked over to the window and tried to open it, hoping the sting of salt air would clear away the cloudy, dreamlike quality of her thoughts. It was stuck. "You'll have to rehang the windows," she said.

"All windows in beach houses do that. The wood swells."

He came up behind her and reached around her to assist with the window. Teale stiffened, but everything within her flared to life. She could feel his warmth surround her, and taste the mild scent of his cologne—sea breezes and masculinity. His pelvis brushed against her buttocks, and his arm encircled hers as he grasped the window sash. She could feel the touch of his chest against her shoulder blades and his gentle indrawn breath. Her nerves tingled with awareness of him, and she thought how easy it would be to sink back into his embrace. She had to fight to keep her muscles rigid.

He lifted the window an inch, but he didn't move away. She felt his breath lightly stirring her hair. "Your hair smells wonderful," he murmured.

If she turned, her lips would meet his and she would be completely lost. So she remained perfectly still. "If you brought me here for the purpose of seduction," she said, managing to inject a note of lightness into her voice, "I think you should know I'm trained in self-defense."

His face brushed against her hair and moved slowly down the shape of her head, luxuriating in the texture. She felt his smile curve against the nape of her neck. "Not very well, I should think, or you'd know better than to let a dangerous felon sneak up on you from behind."

Her breath was coming rapidly, and she braced her hands against the window sill. "Are you dangerous, David?"

His hands came to rest upon her waist, lightly caressing, and with the movement gently tugging her blouse from her waistband. "What do you think?"

His hand slipped beneath the material, light butterfly touches that moulded the pliant flesh of her waist and danced over the shape of her ribs. She couldn't move, her chest ached with the effort of keeping her breathing steady, and her heart thundered so she thought surely he could feel its pressure shaking her ribs. *No,* she thought, somewhat desperately. *No, you can't let this happen.* While another part of her, a deeper, softer, more demanding part whispered, *Yes....*

She brought her hands to his wrist, but could do no more than rest her fingertips there, feeling the strong bones and the light dusting of hair on his forearms. His hands had moved upward so they rested just beneath the band of her bra, but went no farther. Her breasts felt full and swollen, aching for that slight upward movement of his fingertips, his cupping hands.

She said steadily, with all the will at her command, "I'm not the kind of woman who can go to bed with any man who crosses her path, David."

The gentle caressing motion of his fingers stopped, and he lifted his head a little. He inquired quietly, "Am I just any man, Teale?"

She closed her eyes against the agony of need, the insistent demands of her clamoring heart. Firmly, she closed her hands around his wrists, moving his hands away. "You know you're not, David," she said.

He stepped away, and the absence of him was like a physical pain. She leaned forward and lifted the window to its full height. A gust of cool air swept through, and she drank it, letting it soothe her fevered cheeks and calm her quivering muscles. Across the marshes the clouds had begun to darken and roll, powerful shifting shapes of beauty and awe.

She turned slowly, bracing herself against the open window. David was watching her, waiting patiently. There was sadness in his eyes.

She met the gentleness of David's gaze and hardened herself against it. "This can't go on," she said evenly. "There's more at stake now than your little cops-and-robbers games. David, *I've got to know the truth*. How long have you been working for Diangelo? What is your relationship with him?"

Again, the peculiar opaqueness came over his eyes, and he responded simply, "I don't know the man."

Something within Teale snapped. "Damn it, David, don't lie to me! I know—"

His hand shot out and grasped her wrist. Anger darkened his eyes, and his face went hard. "Don't ever say that again," he commanded harshly. "I've made a career out of lying, and if I wanted to do it now I'd do it so well you'd never find out. But I have never lied to you." His hand tightened on her wrist, painfully, and his eyes blazed with low cold fire very close to hers. "Do you understand that? I will never lie to you!"

Teale stared at him, her breath caught in her chest, tendrils of shock and a little bit of fear tracing through her. She tugged experimentally at her wrist. "That hurts," she said.

He released her wrist abruptly, and half turned away. Tension radiated from the set of his shoulders and the cords of his neck. "I'm sorry," he said stiffly.

She rubbed her wrist absently, her breath coming back in shaky waves. David's voice came to her quietly.

"I never planned for this to happen," he said, without turning to look at her. "It's as hard for me as it is for you. You think you're taking a risk by being with me?" She saw the corner of his lips curve downward in a dry, self-mocking smile. "Compared to the chances I'm taking, you don't know what risk is."

Still he didn't turn. He spoke quietly, almost to himself. At times Teale had to strain to catch the words over the sound of the rising wind. "I've spent a lifetime running from one adventure to the other, filling up the spaces, being good at what I did because that was all I knew. I've been shot at in the Sudan, kidnapped in Ireland, lost in the jungles of South America with assassins on my trail. I've had to talk myself out of a blind alley while looking down the barrel of an Uzi and nobody spoke English but me; I've been pistol-whipped, firebombed, jailed. And none of it mattered, nothing bothered me, because it was all just a game.''

He made a small sound, the ghost of a laugh, and shook his head slightly. He turned to face her, and his expression was quiet, naked with the unadorned truth. "Now, I've finally found something real, something worth staying for, believing in, and it has to be you."

Tears were hot in her chest, tears of longing and pain and the need to reach out to him, to comfort him, to reassure him, to simply hold him. But she shook her head, violently. "David, you don't know what you're saying—what you're asking." Her voice was thick and muffled, strained with the effort to keep the tears at bay. "It doesn't matter what you feel, what I feel. It can't be, don't you see that? We're only going to cause...more pain if we let this go on. I am what I am, and you—"

"What am I?" He took a step forward, his voice intent, his movements taut and restrained. "Look at me, Teale, and tell me what you see. Is it really so bad?''

Helplessly, she lifted her eyes to him. What did she see? A man of quiet strength and sincerity, of warmth and tenderness and sensitivity, a man who could look at her and make her believe there were no secrets, who made her want to crawl into his arms and stay there forever.... A gentle man, a solid man. A good man.

She closed her eyes fiercely, trying to blot out the impression. She tried to swallow the tears but her throat only thickened with them. "Do you think it's that easy?" she cried. "Do you think the line between right and wrong is so easily blurred? Damn it, David, I've *got* to believe in the strength of that line—it's all I know, all I have!"

Her fists clenched at her sides, unconsciously infusing strength into her tone. Her eyes pleaded with him to understand. "If I say gambling is all right because it doesn't hurt anyone, why can't I say murder is all right as long as the victim deserved to be killed? If I overlook your activities because they appear to be harmless, then I have to overlook an entire syndicate of drugs and prostitution and graft and corruption because that is what you represent and *that's* where your so-called innocent money is going. Don't you understand that? There is no middle ground for me!"

He said quietly, "I do understand, Teale. I know what you've been through, I know the guilt that drives you to be the best. I know how terrified you are of making a mistake. But listen to me."

He came toward her slowly, and when less than a foot separated them he lifted his hands and clasped her arms, lightly at first and then with more intensity. "I am not a part of syndicated crime," he said clearly, with quiet force. His eyes burned with a low intense light that seemed to want to bore its way into her very soul. "I am not working for or with Diangelo. None of my money will ever find its way into his hands or into those of anyone like him." His fingers dug into her flesh, as though he could physically impart the truth of his words to her. "Believe me, Teale," he said in a low voice. "You have to believe me."

She wanted to believe him. Her soul, her mind, her body ached to believe him. She looked at him helplessly.

"Have you learned to listen to your instincts, Teale?" he demanded softly. "What do your instincts tell you about me?"

She remembered the look on her father's face. *You do believe me, don't you, Teale? You're my daughter, you must believe me.* She remembered the agonizing war between instinct and logic; she remembered the course on which her choice had finally taken her. Had she learned to listen to her instincts? Could she risk making the same mistake again?

Her eyes blurred, and her mouth and her nose were thick with moisture. She looked at David, and she knew what her instincts told her. And if it was a mistake, it was too late to turn away from it now.

"I believe you," she whispered, and she went into his arms.

It was as simple as that.

Eight

They stayed together for a long time, saying nothing, just holding each other. The problems, the complications, the uncertainties dissolved into the simple inevitability of the truth, a truth that had been there all along but that Teale had simply refused to see. The wind gusted through the window and tugged at her skirt. Thunder cracked on a distant shore, but in David's arms she was safe, at peace in the eye of the storm.

"Oh, David," she sighed. "The minute I walked into that party and saw you I knew I was in over my head."

His hands caressed her shoulder blades. "Funny," he said huskily. "I thought exactly the same thing, the first time I saw you."

Teale leaned away from him, tilting her face up to study him. Lightly she traced the shape of his face with

her fingertips, brushing at the hair that fell over his
forehead, smoothing his eyebrows and the satiny flesh
across his cheekbones. She filled her eyes with him,
memorizing details against that time when he might no
longer be there to touch.

"In another lifetime," she whispered, "I could have
loved you...."

His fingers cupped her chin, lifted her face even
closer to his. His eyes were dark and filled to brim-
ming with quiet, certain emotions. "In another lifetime," he answered softly, "I did, and still do."

Their lips met and melded, drawing from each
other, tasting and stroking and caressing, fanning the
fires of passion that had smoldered too long un-
quenched. When their mouths parted both were left
shaken and deeply moved, but the final shreds of uncertainty were gone; there were no more questions to
be asked.

Teale stepped away from him and looked at him for
a long time. Then she laced her fingers through his and
held them tightly. Her gaze didn't waver. "Why don't
you show me the bedroom?" she suggested softly.

Afterward, she couldn't have said whether the bedroom was light or dark, what its colors were or anything at all about it. She saw only David. She turned
to him in the center of the room, and when he would
have gathered her close, she stayed him with a gently
uplifted hand. They had waited so long; they had
fought past so many barriers. Now there was nothing
left to hide, nothing to hold back, and she wanted to
make it last.

Beginning with his face, her hands drifted down
over his body, exploring him by touch, absorbing and
memorizing him with her fingertips. The soft, full

shape of his lips, the coarse texture of his jaw, the dip of his chin. The smooth, heated texture of his skin, the supple column of his neck.

She watched his eyes darken and change as she caressed the breadth of his shoulders, the soft cotton that covered his chest. Her fingertips flowed over his muscles, and his breath caught as she discovered his nipple and made it hard. The shape of his waist, the flat plane of his back. His hips, the firm shape of his buttocks and, below the hem of his shorts, the strong muscles of his lightly furred thighs. Her hands traveled upward and felt the power of his desire. The blaze of yearning she saw in his eyes filled her with pleasure and need.

He gently tugged apart the buttons of her blouse, and she shrugged it off her shoulders. He stroked the bare flesh of her arms, making it prickle with heat and awareness, and his eyes moved over her hungrily. "You are lovely," he said huskily.

"No," she whispered. "I'm not."

"Yes, you are." He leaned forward and pressed his lips against the curve of her collarbone. "Because you're mine."

His mouth covered her breast, dampening the material of her bra with heat and moisture, making her moan out loud. His fingers loosened the clasp of her skirt, and she stepped out of it.

He closed his hands around her buttocks, pressing her to him, and she slipped her hands beneath his shirt, moving upward over his back and around to his ribs and the soft mat of hair on his chest. Her open mouth touched his in a delicate dance of desire, darting tongues and probing explorations, sweet, searching, intense.

She pushed his shirt upward, over his head; in a haze of movements he was released from it and came to her again, his naked chest against her breasts, his abdomen pressing hers. His hands stroked her bare back and circled downward, caressing her thighs, tracing upward to the scrap of nylon that shielded her from him. A knot of longing wound inside her stomach and blossomed at the touch of his hand, and she moaned out loud.

In a single motion he wrapped his arms around her and lifted her to the bed. Above her his face was a blur of beauty and dazed wonder as he placed a kiss upon the corner of her lips and moved to her ear. Her fingers grasped his shoulders as her dizzied awareness darted from the sensation his lips drew against her skin to the exploring motion of his hands upon her legs and her waist. His hand slipped beneath the thin fabric that covered her, then moved lower, fingers seeking and finding her, drawing a breathless, urgent response.

He whispered, "Teale..." His eyes were intent, adoring, absorbing.

She lifted herself against him, wrapping her arms around his neck. She pressed her knee against his hip while the other leg traced his outline upward, and she whispered, "Yes, David, yes."

She didn't know when the last barriers of clothing were removed, only the sensation of his naked thighs brushing hers, the heat of his body melting into hers. Teale could see the tremor in his arm muscles as he held himself above her, the seriousness beneath the soft light in his eyes, the quiet vulnerability that gentled the planes of his face. Her heart swelled with adoration, with trust—with completion. "David," she

whispered, and there was wonder in simply saying his
name. "David...."

She touched the strands of hair that fell forward and
found his face damp with perspiration. His hand was
unsteady as it touched her cheek, brushing her tem-
ple, caressing the shape of her parted lips. She trem-
bled for him.

Then his hands slipped beneath her, his weight eas-
ing from her as firm fingers cupped her buttocks and
lifted her upward. Her breath faded, and her heart
paused, suspended in rapture, as he lowered himself
into her, filling her with a slow ecstatic pressure that
stretched the very boundaries of pleasure to its limits.

Thunder rolled and gathered and rolled again, rat-
tling the windowpanes and shuddering through the
very foundations of the house. The wind exploded in
a rush, flinging hard pellets of rain against the windows. Teale noticed none of it. Locked in the power
of David's embrace, swept away on the rhythms they
created together, for her the universe began and ended
within his arms.

With slow, languorous caresses, they treasured and
explored; with swift, arching thrusts they sought and
discovered, and they hungered for even more. The
storm that raged outside was insignificant in comparison to the storm that grew within them and swept
them away, building and gathering intensity and
pushing them to the very edge of agony... and wonder. It was long, it was loving; it was fierce, and it was
primal, and then the world shattered and exploded
upon itself, forging them together, leaving them weak
and dazed and clinging to each other in the aftermath
of the storm.

They lay together, their perspiration-slick limbs entwined, listening to the sounds of their own unsteady breathing and the roar of the rain against the roof. All this time, Teale thought in stunned and distant wonder, I never knew it could be like this. All the time we were meant to be together, waiting to find each other.... For he was still a part of her, absorbed into every cell of her body and every fiber of her soul. David. Hers.

He bent his head, and his lips brushed her damp hair. "I knew," he whispered, almost as though in response to her thoughts. "I knew it was meant to be like this ... you and me, together. I'm so glad I found you."

Her hand tightened against his chest. "I love you, David."

She felt his breath, deep and slow, as though from joy or wonder. His arms tightened around her. "I have loved you, Teale," he said huskily, "forever."

A beauty filled her, happiness expanding inside her chest and thickening her throat. The only way such wonder could find expression was in a low, gurgling laugh. She lifted her face to him and teased, "Despite all those other women?"

He smiled, lightly tracing her nose from brow to tip with his finger. "There were no other women. It was all just a cover. I also," he told her, "love your eyebrows." And to prove it he kissed each one separately.

She snuggled into his arms, so at peace, so safe while the storm pounded outside, that she couldn't remember a time when she hadn't felt this way. She felt as though it would last forever, this warmth, this love, this simple rightness, and that she would never be threatened again.

David rested his head on the pillow beside her, and he said, "Well, what do you think?"

She looked at him inquiringly.

"Should I buy the house?"

She laughed, low in her throat. "I think you're going to have to," she murmured. "We left the window open in the other room, and you probably have an entire carpet to replace by now."

His hand smoothed her brow with delicate, repeated strokes. "Tomorrow we can pick out new carpet together. I don't intend to live here alone," he said quietly.

And there it was, reality creeping back. The feeling wouldn't last forever. The peace, the simplicity, the certain choices, already they were being threatened.

She turned onto her back, her hands tightening on the sheet at her chest, and opened her eyes to the ceiling. "Do you know," she asked softly, "what frightens me most about my work? Doors. They're every cop's nightmare, I suppose. You walk through a door, you never know what's behind it. The sweat breaks out, your adrenaline starts pumping, you want to shoot at anything that moves, you hear noises, your nerves are screaming. Every time I go through a door I think if I make it out of this one alive, I'll never do it again."

David's arm tightened around her in silent understanding. Teale released a slow breath and closed her eyes. "That's what the future looks like to me now, David. A series of doors. And I'm so scared."

He gathered her into his arms, he pressed a long lingering kiss upon her forehead. "Ah, Teale," he whispered. "You don't know how much I wish I could make it easier for you. But please, just hold on for a little while longer. And trust me. I promise it's going to be all right."

Teale wrapped her arms around him and held him tightly. She wanted to believe. For tonight, if no more, she wanted to believe that somehow, magically, everything was going to be all right. But she knew that in the days ahead she was going to have to be braver than she had ever been in her life.

They didn't leave the marsh house until dawn. Standing on the deck, watching the still white mist rise from the marshes, leaning back into David's embrace and sharing the contented silence only lovers know, Teale could actually imagine herself living here with him. She could imagine quiet days and long nights like the one that had just passed, and David's smile, David's voice, David's touch, filling up her hours for the rest of her life.

He kissed her one last time on the pier before she got into her car. No one was there to see but the gulls and the sun rising by golden inches over the water, but Teale wouldn't have cared at that moment if the entire Bretton Falls Police Department had been there to bear witness to what she had found with David.

"Will I see you tonight?" he asked. His eyes, as he looked down at her, had taken on the silvery reflection of the sun, and Teale thought she had never seen anything more beautiful than the eyes of her lover looking at her.

"Yes," she responded, without hesitation.

He touched her face lightly, and though he smiled there was a trace of wistfulness to it. "You look happy," he said softly. "Stay that way, all right?"

Teale nodded, and at that moment she had no doubt she could make the happiness last.

She went home to shower and change, and despite the lack of sleep, she felt renewed as she drove to work. The storm had washed the world and left it sparkling. The air was clear and bright, and the sky was a blinding blue; sunshine danced off the asphalt and bounced from rooftops, and Teale's mood was just as buoyant. She had an idea.

She strode into the squad room and motioned Sam to follow her into the Captain's office. Sam commented suspiciously, "The last time I saw you looking this smug was when we broke the Harris case. Don't tell me Carey up and turned himself in?"

"Just shut up and listen."

She knocked on the door and received permission to enter. Captain Hollis was standing by the window, watering a stubborn, wilting philodendron. "Damn thing," he muttered without turning. "If I wasn't afraid my wife'd find out I'd pitch the thing through the window... She thought the office needed cheering up. Well, this sure cheers it up, doesn't it?" He plucked off a yellow leaf and tucked it into his pocket.

"Captain," Teale began without preamble, "what kind of deal do you think we could cut David Carey?"

Sam stared at her.

Hollis waved a dismissing hand, busily pruning his plant. "Talk to the D.A. What makes you think Carey can be turned?"

"He can," she answered confidently, and the suspicion in Sam's eyes darkened.

Hollis turned, looking at her for a moment speculatively. "Can he give us Diangelo?"

"I don't think that he's any closer to Diangelo than we are," she said carefully. "But he wants out. And he just might be able to help us wrap up this case."

Hollis frowned and turned back to the plant. "Don't come to me with a lot of ifs and mights. Bring me something to work with."

"Then I have your permission to talk to him?"

Hollis grunted an affirmative. "Damn thing." He plucked off another leaf. "Give it sun, water, plant food—do you think that's enough? No, it still wants more. A lot like my wife."

"I'll keep you informed, sir."

"Saunders."

Teale turned at the door to find Captain Hollis looking at her sternly—and perhaps a bit too perceptively. "You be damn sure you know what you're doing."

"Yes, sir." Teale quickly left the office.

"And just what the hell was that all about?" Sam demanded in an undertone, keeping step with her. "You know how close Carey is to Diangelo—"

"We don't know anything," Teale interrupted firmly.

"We agreed—"

"We were wrong."

Sam stopped and looked at her. "You were with him last night, weren't you?" he demanded quietly.

A flush crawled over her cheeks, and she couldn't meet Sam's eyes. She went over to her desk, and he followed her. "I'm sorry, Sam," she said, for that was the least she owed her partner for the lie. Then she firmly resumed a businesslike demeanor. "But you know we were getting nowhere with the wire—it was a joke. I had to show him some respect. It was the only way I could ever get his trust."

Sam's expression was sober and disappointed and very worried. "He's getting to you, isn't he?"

Teale sat down at her desk and opened a drawer. She drew out a stack of forms she had no intention of filling out and pretended to rearrange them.

"All right," Sam said quietly, after a time. "You're a grown woman, I can't run your life for you. But listen to me."

He sat on the edge of her desk and leaned close. Teale was forced to look up at him. "You're no rookie, Teale," he said levelly. "You know better than this. A man like David Carey has been in this business too long and has gotten too good at it to turn over a new leaf now. Oh, I'm not saying he won't cop a plea to get out of this one—if the D.A. will even deal with him, which I very much doubt—but that's all it will be. Just another narrow escape for him. Don't go talking yourself into thinking you can save the man's soul, because you can't."

For just a moment reality crept back in, and with it despair. She looked at Sam, trying to fight back helplessness with bravado. "I've got to try," she said stubbornly. But even as she spoke she knew the odds were against her, and a note of pleading softened her voice. "Sam, I've got to *try*."

Of course, Teale knew she was fighting a losing battle. As the day crawled by she began to think, she began to sober, she began to realize what she was up against. The lovely euphoric glow in the pit of her stomach dissolved into a faint uneasy doubt, and the

rosy haze that had enveloped her since the previous
night gradually began to melt away. Suspicion reared
its head once or twice, and it was all she could do to
fight it down. She started to feel like a cop again.

The evidence was stacked against David. Years of
careless crime, notorious connections through his
family, records that had been doctored by someone
very powerful. David was an extraordinarily clever,
resourceful man. He had said from the beginning that
he intended to keep an eye on her and that was exactly what he had done. He had kept her constantly in
sight, he had monitored her every move, he had made
certain her investigation went nowhere. He had be-
haved exactly like a man who had too much at stake
to let anyone get in the way. What made her think that
he would abandon it all now? He had made many
promises; reformation was not among them.

And he had never claimed to be an innocent man.

Then she had to ask herself the harshest question of
all. What if David refused to turn? What if he were
more involved than he had admitted? What if he
couldn't or wouldn't leave it behind? What if, Teale,
she demanded of herself, your choice is between
sending David to jail and running away with him to
live a life of crime? What will you do then?

What frightened her was that she didn't know the
answer.

Oh, David, she thought bleakly, How could this
have happened? Why did it have to be you? It had all
seemed so simple in the isolated house on the marsh.
It had all seemed so clear, basking in the glow of his
love. But throughout the day, David never called, and
in the real world nothing was simple at all.

She left the office at four o'clock, and no one objected or questioned. When she pulled into the parking lot a red Porsche was parked in the space next to hers.

Her heart was thumping with a quivery, schoolgirlish uncertainty as she went up the sidewalk. Joy because she was going to see her lover, and dread because she was afraid it might be for the last time. It's simple, Teale, she told herself. Present it to him like you would to any other suspect. Ask him if he'd be willing to turn state's evidence in exchange for immunity. See what he's got to offer. He'll cooperate, you know he will. It's the only way.

Teale entered her apartment, and David was stretched out on her sofa, sound asleep. She stopped on the threshold, caught by the wave of tenderness and affection that washed over her. The doubts and dark suspicions that had haunted her all day evaporated into nothing more than paranoid fantasy as she looked at the man she loved. He looked so vulnerable in his sleep, the lines of his face relaxed and innocent, the strong lithe body defenseless and at ease. She walked silently over to the sofa and knelt beside him, lightly smoothing away the lock of hair that shadowed his forehead.

He awoke like a soldier, she thought, instantly alert. His hand shot out to grab her wrist, his muscles stiffened for self-defense, like one so deeply ingrained against unexpected attacks that preventing them was second nature to him. His reaction startled Teale, then puzzled her, connecting in some odd way to something that didn't fit the image she had of David at all, something that bore further investigation.

But in less than a heartbeat the swift hardness in David's eyes faded into a drowsy smile, his hand relaxed on her wrist, and he sank back against the cushion. "I can't believe I fell asleep," he murmured ruefully. "And I was trying so hard to impress you."

"You also," Teale informed him softly, smiling as she smoothed back his hair, "broke into my apartment."

"Lockpicking is my specialty. *That* should impress you."

The hazy, slumberous light in his eyes was soft and sensuous and his gaze travelled over her face, resting on each individual feature like a caress. He lifted his hand, lightly tracing the shape of her ear with his fingertip, making her shiver with the sensation.

"I could get used to waking up with you," he said huskily.

Teale smiled, feeling the warmth of his gaze, the butterfly touch of his fingertips go through her like a slow, lazy wave, opening her pores, tingling her nerve endings, evoking an immediate and thorough response. "What are you doing here? Besides sleeping, of course."

"I came armed with all the makings of an unforgettable dinner, knowing that you'd forgive me for breaking into your apartment when you tasted my very special spaghetti sauce."

"I hate spaghetti." She leaned forward and lightly brushed his lips with hers.

"Not the way I make it you don't." She saw his pupils dilate with slow arousal, and he cupped his hand around her head, holding her face a few inches before his. His voice was low and thick. "Of course, it may be too late to start the sauce now."

"That's what you get for falling asleep."

He closed the distance between their two mouths with his tongue, gently tasting the outline of her lips, teasing, moistening.

"I had a hard day," he murmured.

"And night."

"And night." His fingers moved downward from her head, cupping and tracing the knobs of her spine. "And I'm not really all that hungry anymore."

She rubbed her cheek against his, feeling the satiny texture and the firm bone and the shadow of his beard against her chin. "Me, either."

"What I really need—" he threaded both hands through her hair and lifted her face above him, his skin flushed with passion, his eyes lazy bright but dark with need "—is a shower. Care to join me?"

Teale smiled and got slowly to her feet, lacing her fingers through his. "My pleasure."

Mesmerized by the warm, enveloping spray of the shower, Teale ran her soapy hands over his shoulders, down the length of his arms, caressing each finger. She smiled up at him through the water that streamed over her face. "Now, isn't this better than slaving over a hot stove?"

"Infinitely." He lifted her arm and drew the soapy sponge down its length, his eyes soft and alive with lazy intent.

Teale thought, We should talk. I can't put it off forever. But just then he drew the sponge down to her breast, softly circling her nipple, and she gasped with pleasure. She tried to concentrate, but her hands moved of their own volition to his waist, caressing the slippery texture of his flesh, sliding down to his thighs. "Tell me about your hard day."

"I've forgotten all about it." He let the sponge drop and replaced it with his fingers, drawing gentle circles on the soapy tips of her breasts. She went weak, and his eyes were alive with pleasure as he watched her. "Tell me about your day, love. I imagine it was much harder than mine."

There, he had given her the opening. Talk to him, Teale.

"I thought about you all day," was all she could manage, and even that was hoarse and weak. Her hands circled around to shape his buttocks, pressing him to her.

He dipped his head, opening her mouth with teasing, darting motions of his tongue. He spread his hands over the small of her back, a slow insistent pressure drawing her close until she felt the hardness and length of his arousal pressing into her stomach. His tongue entered her slowly, thoroughly, tasting of fresh water, musky warmth and David.

Desire blossomed throughout her body, tingling in her fingertips, aching in her stomach, melting with liquid, pulsating warmth. The spray of the shower was a distant hum that was drowned out by the beat of her heart and the heavy, unsteady rush of David's breathing, and her own.

He lifted his face, stroking her back, her shoulders and her thighs with long liquid caresses. She clung to him, her neck arched to receive the kiss he placed at the edge of her collarbone. His hand slipped between her thighs, caressing, stroking, opening her. His eyes were intent upon her face, watching and absorbing her. Teale shuddered and moaned with pleasure as he slipped a finger inside her.

Instinctively she pressed against him, relying upon the strong support of his hand on her back as her knee caressed his thigh and his hip. Then she felt his hands beneath her, pressing her against the slippery length of his body, lifting her. Her knees encircled his waist, and she gasped and lost all reason as she felt the swollen tip of his masculinity pressing against her. Her breath stopped, her heart roared, everything within her was suspended and bursting as the pressure increased, stretching and aching, and slowly his full length slid into her.

Her muscles convulsed. She clasped him to her, and dimly she thought she cried out as the shudders over-took her in powerful, wracking waves. It seemed to last forever; it left her stunned and weak and clinging to him helplessly, needing him as she needed her very life's breath.

She barely knew when he lifted her in his arms and carried her, naked, to the bedroom. He dried her body with a towel, and his face was a blur of tenderness and adoration above her. She drew him to her again, and they made love with slow, languorous perfection while the afternoon faded away and twilight settled upon them like a benediction. It can't be wrong, she thought distantly, filled with the contentment of his love, not when it feels so right....

She didn't talk to David that night. There would be plenty of time.

Nine

Time ran out abruptly the next morning.

Captain Hollis was waiting for her when she came in. Silently, he motioned Teale and Sam into his office and closed the door. He stepped behind the desk, took out a file and tossed the folder onto the center of his desk. "This is your new assignment," he said. "A series of pharmaceutical thefts—Quaaludes seem to be the most popular item, although they're also making quite a killing in amphetamines. Obviously a fairly organized gang, but not particularly bright. The three stores they've hit this week have all been within a four-block radius."

Teale stared at him, disbelieving. It was Sam who spoke first.

"Wait a minute—what about Carey?"

"It's over," Hollis said flatly.

A thumping started in Teale's chest, and it seemed to be affecting the quality of her breathing. Dread tightened in her stomach as she struggled to find her voice. "What do you mean 'over'? Has there been a break? An...arrest?" *Impossible*, she thought. David had left her no more than three hours ago. If anything were about to break she would have known, he would have known.

"I mean it's over," Hollis said shortly. "We're getting nowhere, and we're dropping the case."

The relief that flooded her made Teale weak and then ill with guilt. David was safe. It was over. But David was wrong, and she was an officer of the law. How was she supposed to feel?

Sam said softly, "Whoa. You don't just walk away from a case because it's getting too tough. What's going on here?"

Captain Hollis's face was tight, but Teale could see the frustration in his eyes. She knew as well as Sam did that he was hiding something. The difference was, she didn't want to know what it was.

"You've got your orders," Hollis responded. "Get busy."

"No, sir," Sam answered with a quiet stubbornness that was his trademark. "Not until you tell us what this is all about."

Sam, shut up, Teale wanted to cry. Leave it alone, it's over! Don't you know when we're well off? But she couldn't say that. She wasn't even sure she meant it.

Sam persisted. "Look, I know it looks like we're stonewalled, but we're working on an angle. Give us a couple more days, a week at the outside—"

"No!" Hollis shouted. The frustration in his eyes snapped into anger. "It's out of my hands, damn it!"

Teale and Sam stared at him, and Hollis took a breath, knowing he had gone too far to let it drop at that. "Look," he said in a moment, more quietly. "I'm just as much in the dark as you are. All I know is that this came straight from the chief of police and our orders are to *back off*."

Sam and Teale left the office in a greatly subdued state. "God," Sam said at last in a low voice. "I hate what I'm thinking."

Teale made herself look at him, hating it as well, perhaps even more. If Diangelo had gotten as far as city hall, if the corruption were that widespread....

She said, "We don't know that." But she kept remembering David's words, *I know how hard it is on you. Just hold on a little longer. It won't be much longer, I promise.*

But no. David couldn't have done this. David didn't have that much power. David wouldn't do this.

There was a sick, hollow feeling in the pit of her stomach and a dim roaring far back in her head. She made herself say, "It could be—the feds could have gotten wind of this, and are taking over. You know how they feel about local departments horning in on their territory."

Sam looked disgusted and not entirely convinced. "That makes me even madder. We do all the work, and the government boys waltz in and snap up the collar."

Then Sam looked at her soberly. "Whatever," he said, "one thing is for sure: whatever Carey's involved in, there's more at stake than a few thousand dollars in poker chips."

Teale swallowed hard. The hollowness in her stomach had grown into a great, yawning gap. "Drugs?" She was surprised at how calmly the word came out.

Sam nodded. "Word on the street is that there's a big shipment due to hit, and soon. That was the new angle I mentioned to Hollis."

She thought, No. David wouldn't lie to me. He told me, he promised me.

Sam thumped the file in his hand with his thumbnail. "Hell, moaning about it's not going to do a damn bit of good. It's out of our hands. You want to take a look at this case?"

Teale was remembering David's face, the look in his eyes as he had kissed her goodbye this morning. He hadn't lied to her. *God, don't let him have lied to me.*

If another arm of the law had stopped the investigation, David was in more trouble than he knew. If David himself had done it . . .

She had to know. She didn't know whether she was going to warn David or confront him, but she had to see him. And she had to see him now.

Her eyes met Sam's. He must have known what she was thinking before she spoke, because swift alarm crossed his face. "No," she said quietly. "You start the new assignment without me. There's something I have to do first."

His voice was sharp, and his hand came out to detain her. "Teale—"

But she pulled away from his grasp almost absently and kept on walking. She didn't look back.

By the time she reached David's beach house a curious calm had overtaken her, a sense of detachment. She wasn't even surprised when she saw the long black car parked in front of David's house, and she didn't even ask herself to whom it belonged. Perhaps on some subconscious level the truth she should have admitted long ago had begun to seep in, and she was in a state of shock. Perhaps she was simply remembering that she was, first and foremost, a cop.

She drove to the end of David's street and parked. Only once, when she got out of the car, did a small desperate voice cry out inside her, Teale, don't do this. Walk away. You don't want to know. But she ignored it.

She walked down to the beach, circling David's house and approaching it from the side. There were a few sunbathers on the beach, but they ignored her. When she was fifty feet from the house, she could hear the murmur of voices. She moved closer, shielded by a bright hedge of bougainvillea that separated David's house from the one next door, and she saw two men on the deck. One of them was David. The other was Diangelo.

The sun was hot on her scalp, the sea breeze was tangy. Inside she felt cool, uninvolved and relaxed. Her heart wasn't even beating fast. Working on instincts as natural as breathing, she moved silently toward them, staying close to the side of the building, and slipped underneath the deck.

Diangelo's voice came to her clearly. "You're a good man, David. I wasn't sure of you at first, but now I think we may have the basis for a relationship."

But David's voice sounded different—hard and coarse, unlike any tone she had ever heard him use before. As though the man who was speaking were not someone she knew at all.

"You just make sure it's top quality," he said. "My clients have contracted for the best, and I can't move junk."

"You have my guarantee. Forty kilos tonight, and we will go from there."

"You'll deliver it personally?"

"I always break in my new men personally. It saves so much misunderstanding later on."

"I like the way you do business."

Diangelo chuckled. "And I like the way you do business. Yes, a clever little scheme you have here. Small town, no competition, not too much attention. Cover it with a little casino action, and the contacts come naturally. We could move millions out of here, David . . . if you're really as good as you say you are."

David answered, "I'm better."

Diangelo laughed and clapped him on the back. Footsteps moved overhead, going into the house. Teale waited until she heard the front door open, and then she climbed the steps to the deck and went through the open door into the dining room.

She heard the front door close, and she sat down at the table. It was cool inside the house, refreshed by the constant sea breeze, and the room was splattered with light. She kept thinking she should feel something—anger, betrayal, horror. She felt nothing at all.

There was a highball glass on the table, and droplets of condensation were beginning to form a ring on the veneered surface. She lifted the glass and tasted it absently. Club soda. She should have known.

When she set the glass down again, David was standing at the threshold of the room.

His eyes were dark, and the line of his jaw was knotted grimly. He had no need to ask how long she had been there or what she had heard. It was all written on her face, and slowly his own expression faded from repressed shock and anger to simple resignation.

He said, after what seemed like a very long time, "I suppose you want an explanation."

Teale studied the pattern the droplets of moisture were forming on the glass. Absently, she gathered a few drops on her fingertips and rubbed the wetness with her thumb. Her voice was very calm and matter-of-fact.

"Did you ever hear the story of the man and the snake, David?"

He said nothing, and she went on casually, "A man was walking through the woods in the wintertime, and he found this snake who had waited too long to go into hibernation. It was frozen stiff, and the man, being softhearted by nature, took pity on it. He took it home, laid it by the fire, thawed it out. He brought it a bowl of warm milk, and the snake drank it down, recovering fast. But when the man reached down to cover the snake with a blanket, to keep it warm, the snake bit him.

"Well, the man was shocked. He said to the snake, 'Why did you do that? I saved your life, I brought you into my home, I thawed you out and I fed you. How could you bite me?' And the snake just looked at him and said, 'You knew I was a snake when you picked me up.'"

Teale raised her eyes from the glass and looked at David. "No, I don't want an explanation," she said quietly. "I'm not surprised, I'm not disappointed. I knew what you were when I picked you up."

The muscle in David's jaw knotted again, just briefly, and there was a flare of something far back in his eyes that could have been hurt. Teale was touched by a dim amazement—almost amusement—that *he* should be angry.

"It's always so simple for you, isn't it, Teale?" he said stiffly.

"Simple," she repeated softly. A pain began just below her rib cage, tugging and tightening, but she ignored it. She couldn't give in to the hurt now, she couldn't acknowledge the agony of betrayal, the crushed dreams, the anger. Because if she did, she would start screaming, and she would never stop.

She met his gaze levelly. "Oh, yes, it was simple. Simple to play with you, simple to flirt with you, simple to fall in love with you. What wasn't simple was believing in you, but I even did that." The pain caught again and twisted. She released an unsteady breath, trying to control it. "You were good, David," she said simply. "You were damn good."

He looked at her searchingly. The lines on his face were taut. "But I wasn't good enough, was I? Because you're still thinking with your head and not your heart, and you never believed in me at all."

She lurched to her feet, and for one brief moment control snapped. "Stop it! Just—" she drew in a breath through her teeth, clearing the fog of rage and hurt with one final, decisive stroke of will "—*stop it*."

"Or maybe," he said softly, "*you* weren't good enough."

She didn't know what he meant, and she didn't want to know. She made herself calm inside; she made herself very, very cold. "It was you who pulled the strings down at city hall to get us off the case, wasn't it?"

For another moment he looked at her intently. She saw the struggle behind his eyes—the anger and the hurt and the longing—and it stirred her. It made her, for a moment, uncertain.

Then, as though forcefully subduing his inner emotions, his face went blank. He answered simply, "Yes. You were getting too close, and I thought it would be easier—on both of us."

A wave of tiredness swept her, and defeat rose up in its wake. She closed her eyes slowly. "I wish you'd done it sooner," she said softly, with an effort. "A lot sooner."

He came toward her, and he took both her arms. His grip was not hard, but it made her look at him. He said quietly, "You should know two things. First, you're not leaving this place unless I want you to. But I guess you knew that when you came in."

She met his eyes without fear. "Yes, I guess I did."

The harsh lines in his face softened, fractionally and just briefly. Then he went on, "Second, you're not nearly as smart as you think you are, Detective Saunders, and at this moment I can't think of a reason in the world why I should give you a second chance. But I'm going to."

His lashes lowered for a moment, obscuring his eyes, and when he looked back at her the anger was gone, and so was the calculated indifference. There was nothing there but resignation. "This might strike you as funny, but there was a time there when I might have given it all up for you. But seeing the way you struggled with your conscience—seeing the devotion you had to your duty and how much you were willing to sacrifice for it—well, it reminded me that I have some honor left, too. Warped though it might be, I've made commitments, too, if only to myself, and I'm going to carry them through. It would be easy for me to blow it all now, Teale, but I'm not going to do it.

"Let me tell you this." His hands tightened on her wrists, and intensity flared in his eyes, dark and low. "I have told you the truth. I have given you all the evidence you need, and if there were anything inside you at all that ever cared for me—if you wanted to believe, even the slightest bit—you would know the truth. That's all I can do. I can't make you love me, and I for damn sure can't make you trust me. It's up to you."

For a moment she wavered. This was David, her David, with whom she had shared intimacy of body, mind and spirit. Deep down inside her something stirred and responded to him and wanted, even now, to believe him. Furiously, determinedly, she fought back the instinct.

And he saw it in her eyes. He released her arms and stepped away, and the sorrow in his eyes was something she would never forget. "I'm sorry, Teale," he said quietly.

She turned and ran from the room.

Ten

Teale didn't remember driving home. She didn't remember opening her door or walking inside or opening the curtains. She must have started to straighten up
the house, an automatic, routine action that was
nothing more than the result of shock, because the
next thing she knew she was in the bedroom, staring
at the rumpled sheets where she and David had lain the
night before, lifting a pillow and bringing it slowly to
her face, inhaling the lingering scent of him.

And then she was sitting on the edge of the bed, her
arms wrapped around herself, doubled over with the
waves of agony that wracked her. It was a physical
thing, clawing at her stomach, knotting her muscles,
cramping in her throat and chest. She couldn't cry.
There was some pain that was too strong for tears. She
could only hold herself and rock back and forth, and

occasionally a dry, harsh sob would be torn from her throat. But the tears wouldn't come.

Visions of David kept stabbing at her. Sleek and sophisticated at the party, bending to kiss her hand. Candlelight dancing in his eyes, the sea breeze tossing his hair. His face flushed with passion above her, gentle in sleep, tight with anger, naked with longing. And now... just now, the sorrow and the disappointment and the hurt when he looked at her.

She had no need to wonder why he had let her go. Nothing she could do would stop him now. He held all the cards. He had planned it perfectly. She knew about Diangelo, and she knew about tonight, but she was powerless. Without backup she couldn't make the bust, and without authority she couldn't make the case. He had nothing to fear from her. He had won.

But he hadn't looked like a man who had won. It haunted her, it tore at her, the look in his eyes when he let her go. Where had she seen that look before?

Her father. That was the way he had looked when he knew she hadn't believed him. It was the look that had haunted her for four years, and she had seen it again today, on David Carey's face.

A sound caught in her throat, harsh and scraping, like a gasp of horror or a choked-off sob. She sat up, slowly pushing a shaking hand through her hair. "Oh, no," she whispered. Her muscles tightened, and she squeezed her eyes shut against it. "Oh, no, don't let this be happening again."

I have given you all the evidence you need, David had said to her. *If you wanted to believe, even the slightest bit, you would know the truth.*

But what truth? What evidence? She wanted to believe him, it seemed at times her entire life and all she had ever valued depended upon believing in him. But what truth?

All the evidence.

Strange things began to come back to her, then; things that didn't entirely make sense. That conversation they had had the night of the storm, when he had told her about his foster father. *It was destroying him,* David had said. *And I was angry. Not that anything I can do makes much difference in the big scheme of things, but it helps to keep my hand in.* That didn't sound like a man who wanted to continue the business that had killed his stepfather. It sounded like someone who wanted to fight it....

She remembered the way he had awakened yesterday, swift, alert, ready for self-defense. Like a soldier, she had thought at the time. And she remembered the other thing that had puzzled her, scraps of a conversation that had been buried beneath her own anxiety and fear of believing. *I've been shot at in the Sudan, lost in the jungles of South America...*

What was David doing in the Sudan? Or South America? Or being kidnapped in Ireland, for that matter? None of it fit his freewheeling playboy image; those were not locations in which a small-time gambler was likely to find himself, or even a big-time operative in a crime syndicate, whose only concerns were profit and loss.

Small things, vague things, things which taken separately would mean nothing. Things which, even in the overview, could be interpreted more than one way.

Have you learned to listen to your instincts, Teale? Have you?

How was it that David had known every move they were going to make before they made it? No one was that smart or that lucky. The sudden orders from the chief's office, the missing records, the blatant gaps in his file.... Who would have the power to erase a man's entire identity at whim? Did even Diangelo's influence reach that high? Was he capable of performing the kinds of things Teale had seen these past weeks?

Perhaps not. But the United States government was.

It wasn't a conscious decision made through logic and the rational processing of facts and information. The empiric skills in which Teale had trained herself so carefully had very little value at that moment. No, the truth came from deep within her, certain and sure, but not explicable even to herself. She simply knew.

She gripped the edge of the mattress to still the tremors in her arms. She was shaking all over. "David Carey, you son of a—" The exclamation was broken off in a gasp, though whether it was a reaction of shock or wonder or sheer joy she could not be sure. She was weak with the power of discovery, and she had to catch her breath.

She brought an unsteady hand to her face, pushing back her hair, and a slow, amazed, slightly rueful smile broke through. "You're one of the good guys!" she whispered.

Teale didn't have a designer gown or borrowed jewels that night, but otherwise the scene at David's beach house was unchanged from the first time she had been there. She wore a simple black sheath so as not to be too conspicuous among the partyers, but she didn't take a chance on being refused admission at the front door. She entered David's house the same way she had that afternoon and for twenty minutes mingled with the guests so as to draw no attention to herself.

She knew she would be recognized, of course—if not by David, then by one of his henchmen—and that, most likely, she would be forcibly escorted away. David had gone to a lot of trouble to avoid local police involvement, and he wouldn't be pleased to find her here tonight. In fact, if she were any kind of professional she would have respected his wishes and stayed away—but she was too much of a woman in love to do that. Not when David's life might be in danger, not when he might need her, not when he didn't know that she was on his side.

David had been clever to disguise the meeting beneath the routine activity of one of his parties. Diangelo would enter by an unobserved door, and David would make sure to hold the meeting out of the way of innocent bystanders. Teale's guess was the secret room. When she tried the handle of the game room and found it locked, she was certain of it.

She stationed herself in the hallway nearby, pretending to check her makeup in her compact mirror. She didn't have to wait long before the mirror reflected someone coming stealthily up behind her. It was the large, blunt-faced man whom David had introduced as George.

"Good evening, George," she said, returning the compact to her evening purse. "You should know two things. First, I'm not about to be thrown out of here. Second, I've got my hand on a .38 special, and I guess you know I can use it."

As she turned she allowed him to see the barrel of the revolver she had hidden in her evening purse, and he stopped, his eyes going dark.

"Now." She spoke quickly, before he could get the wrong impression, but she kept her tone pleasant. "I want you to take me into that room with David and Diangelo. Very quietly, very casually. I'm not going to make a fuss. But if David needs any help I'm going to be there to give it to him, do you understand?"

He didn't look as though he was sure he did, but when she moved her purse a fraction, he had no choice. "I guess my partner underestimated you," he said lowly.

"No," she said, and a shadow of sadness almost blurred her concentration. "For a while there, he might have *over*estimated me. But I'm not going to disappoint him again. Come on, George. I'll stay out of the way, I promise. But if you don't take me to him, I'm going to make a scene like none you've ever seen, and that will be *sure* to blow the deal. So let's go."

"Lady," he said sourly, "you are more trouble than you're worth. I tried to tell him that from the beginning."

But George was taking out a key and moving toward the door, and Teale smiled. "I'm glad he didn't listen."

There were three men in the room besides David. Diangelo was seated at a card table, and two men, whom Teale took to be his bodyguards, flanked him. David was standing on the other side of the table. Open on the table between them were two briefcases, containing more packets of cocaine than Teale had ever seen in her life.

The reaction to her entry was immediate and alarming. Diangelo's eyes sharpened and narrowed; the two men beside him reached inside their coats. David turned, his face hard, his eyes dark with shock

and fury. Their gazes held for an instant—no more—
and with all the power in her soul Teale tried to com-
municate the truth to him.

David lifted a mild hand and half turned to the three
men. "Gentlemen, you know my partner, George.
And this—" he extended his hand backward for Teale
"—is just my woman. I'm thinking of keeping her
around for a while; she might as well get used to the
action."

Teale went to David, relaxing her grip on her evening bag fractionally. David's arm went around her
tightly, almost protectively. He was still angry, but
Teale had expected that. It's going to be all right, David, she thought. I promise.

Diangelo chuckled, and the men beside him relaxed. "You sure do things in a funny way, Carey.
Either you're a sloppy fool or too damn confident for
your own good—I haven't figured it out yet. But it
won't take long. If you're a fool, you'll end up dead.
If you're really as good as you think you are, well, like
I said, we'll see."

His eyes wandered to Teale, stripping her up and
down. David's arm tightened on her waist.

"Hell," Diangelo said, "let her stay. Let's just get
this over with. I've got other appointments."

David reached down and took a briefcase from un-
der the table. He snapped the locks and set it before
Diangelo. It was filled with money. "There you are.
Take your time counting it."

Diangelo looked at him shrewdly. "You can be
damn sure I will."

"Meanwhile," David took a small, almost casual
step to the side, keeping Teale in back of him, and in

the same motion he pulled a revolver from inside his jacket. "You're busted. FBI."

Teale whipped out her weapon from her purse and leveled it at Diangelo. Diangelo started to rise and George drew on him from the side. The sliding panel of the mural wall snapped open, and the room was filled with federal agents.

The next few moments were a blur. People were everywhere, tension was high, movement was constant. Teale didn't know how many people she explained her presence to, she didn't even count how many agents filled the house. She did know that at some point she lost sight of David.

When she found him again, they were taking Diangelo away. David was a shadow on the back deck, standing with his arms braced against the railing, looking out over the sea. Teale left the noise and confusion and stepped out onto the deck, sliding the door firmly closed behind her.

She could see the tension in his shoulders and the cords of his neck; she could feel it radiating from him in waves. She knew how it was. The adrenaline high that followed a bust, the singing nerves, the frantic plunges between euphoria and despair. She did not speak for a time, and when she did it was very softly.

"Are you mad?"

"Damn right I'm mad." His voice was harsh, and he didn't look at her. "You could have been killed. You could have gotten me killed. You could have blown the bust. And to think I argued for letting the locals in on this."

"Did you really?"

"Of course I did," he snapped. "After I met you ... hell, it doesn't matter. They were right. Working with local authorities has never been anything but trouble."

"I know," she said quietly. "And I'm sorry. I knew I was taking chances and it was unprofessional . . . but I couldn't let you face it alone."

For a moment, just a moment longer, she thought she had lost him. Her entire soul and all she had ever cared about in the world, seemed suspended in the agonizing silence between one heartbeat and the next. And then he took a breath and spoke again, slowly. "What changed your mind?" He still didn't look at her.

She took her time forming a reply, and when she did it was another question. "Why didn't you throw me out?"

Slowly she felt some of the tension leave his shoulders, and he made a soft sound that almost could have been a laugh. "I should have, I suppose. You scared me out of five good years."

Hope soared, cautious but brilliant. She touched his arm, lightly. "But you knew I wouldn't betray you."

He turned to her. His eyes were bright, electric and intense. "Yes," he said quietly. "That much I did know."

His eyes searched her face, hungrily, and she knew he was going to kiss her. She wanted him to kiss her, with all the desperation in her soul.

But he merely took another calming breath and deliberately did not touch her. "So," he said, and his tone was almost neutral. "I guess the cop in you finally put the pieces together."

"No." She shook her head, holding him with her eyes, pleading with him to understand. "The woman did. David, I'm sorry," she went on in a rush. "I'm sorry for the trouble I caused, for the things I said, for not being grown-up enough to trust my own emotions, for not believing you."

He lifted his hand and lightly touched her hair. She saw the change come over his eyes, a softening and a welcome, and her heart swelled. "For the trouble you caused," he said, "we have a jurisdictional dispute to thank. For the rest...well, we're working on that, aren't we?"

She nodded and went into his arms. For a long time they simply held each other, drawing comfort, soaring with relief, forming quiet promises. Then, abruptly, Teale pushed away.

"I could strangle you for what you put me through," she said angrily. "Why didn't you tell me?"

"I was under cover, too," he reminded her. "And under orders. The whole operation depended on its going down just like we had mapped it, and I don't mind telling you, you gave us a few bad moments."

"I know that. But later, after we... David, you could have told me then! How could you put me through that?"

The lines around his eyes were strained, and he clasped her hands, warmly, but with pressure that suggested he was afraid she might even now slip away. "Teale, I tried every way I could to tell you without compromising my integrity or the operation. You had a job to do, too, and I couldn't ask you to just back away on my word alone. At some point you had to

either believe me or not. I know it was asking a lot.
Probably too much. But it was the only thing I could
do."

He dropped his gaze. "And by this afternoon... I
should have told you then. But I was so hurt. After all
we'd been through—finding you like that, seeing you
look at me with such disgust in your eyes—it was a
shock. And I guess I figured that if I couldn't have
your trust voluntarily I didn't want it at all."

"David," she said softly. "You took an awful
chance. If I had gone to the department with what I
knew— We might not have been able to make a bust,
but we could have blown your whole operation."

He nodded soberly. "I guess my superiors—if I ever
tell them—would consider that a drastic error in
judgment. But I haven't been thinking too clearly since
I met you. And somehow I knew you wouldn't go to
the department."

"I should have."

"Yes, you should have. I guess both of us have been
acting a little less like cops than we should. It takes
something very powerful to overcome that many years
of training, Teale."

"I'm glad," she whispered, "that we found it."

She lifted her face to him, and they kissed. Their
joining was long and lingering and full of promise,
and when they parted they knew it was only the beginning.

David stroked her hair. "What I said this afternoon, Teale, I meant it. There were times during this
last operation when I came closer to blowing it than I
ever had in my life. I came into it pretty burned out, I

guess, and I was ready to quit. But knowing you gave me back something of myself, the parts I thought I had lost. Thank you for that, Teale.''

"You've given me something, too, David. With my father... something inside me was crippled, and I thought I'd never get over it. But this time—" she smiled at him, faintly, and touched her fingers to his face "—I got it right. That makes it better, some-how.''

He drew her into his arms again, and she lay still and content against the beat of his heart.

"I'm taking a year off," he said, after a time, "to rest and regroup, and maybe find out what it feels like to be a real person for a change, instead of always playing an undercover role.''

Teale nodded against his shoulder. "What have you decided to do about the house?''

"I close the deal in thirty days." His finger touched her chin, tipping her head back to look at him. His eyes were dark and sincere. "But I told you once I don't intend to live there alone.''

Teale's heart was thumping erratically. "Is that a proposal?''

"No. This is. Teale," he said softly, "will you marry me?''

Her eyes searched his face, hardly daring to believe the love she saw there or the happiness that swelled her own heart. "It's a very important decision, choosing a partner.''

"Yes," he agreed soberly. "My life will be in your hands—and yours in mine.''

"I can't think of anywhere else I'd rather place my life," she whispered.

"Nor I, mine."

He drew her into his arms again, and she came willingly, holding on to him, sharing a kiss that sealed a promise.

After a long time they turned and, arms entwined, went back into the empty house.

* * * * *

Silhouette Intimate Moments

Rx: One Dose of

```
┌─────────────────────────────┐
│                             │
│            DODD             │
│          MEMORIAL           │
│          HOSPITAL           │
│                             │
└─────────────────────────────┘
```

In sickness and in health the employees of Dodd Memorial Hospital stick together, sharing triumphs and defeats, and sometimes their hearts as well. Revisit these special people next month in the newest book in Lucy Hamilton's Dodd Memorial Hospital Trilogy, *After Midnight*—IM #237, the time when romance begins.

Thea Stevens knew there was no room for a man in her life—she had a young daughter to care for and a demanding new job as the hospital's media coordinator. But then Luke Adams walked through the door, and everything changed. She had never met a man like him before—handsome enough to be the movie star he was, yet thoughtful, considerate and absolutely determined to get the one thing he wanted—Thea.

Finish the trilogy in July with *Heartbeats*—IM #245.

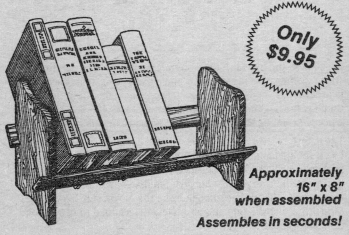

Silhouette Desire

COMING NEXT MONTH

#421 LOVE POTION—Jennifer Greene
Dr. Grey Treveran didn't believe in magic until he was rescued by the bewitching Jill Stanton. She taught him how to dream again, and he taught her how to love.

#422 ABOUT LAST NIGHT...—Nancy Gramm
Enterprising Kate Connors only had one obstacle in the way of her cleanup campaign—Mitch Blake. Then their heated battle gave way to passion....

#423 HONEYMOON HOTEL—Sally Goldenbaum
Sydney Hanover needed a million dollars in thirty days to save Candlewick Inn. She tried to tell herself that Brian Hennesy was foe, not friend, but her heart wouldn't listen.

#424 FIT TO BE TIED—Joan Johnston
Jennifer Smith and Matthew Benson were tied together to prove a point, but before their thirty days were up, Matthew found himself wishing their temporary ties were anything but!

#425 A PLACE IN YOUR HEART—Amanda Lee
Jordan Callahan was keeping a secret from Lisa Patterson. He wanted more than their past friendship now, but could the truth destroy his dreams?

#426 TOGETHER AGAIN—Ariel Berk
Six years before, past events had driven Keith LaMotte and Annie Jameson apart. They'd both made mistakes; now they had to forgive each other before they could be...together again.

AVAILABLE NOW:

Silhouette Special Edition

NORA ROBERTS'S 50TH SILHOUETTE NOVEL

In May, SILHOUETTE SPECIAL EDITION celebrates Nora Roberts's "golden anniversary"— her 50th Silhouette novel!

The Last Honest Woman launches a three-book "family portrait" of entrancing triplet sisters. You'll fall in love with all THE O'HURLEYS!

The Last Honest Woman—May
Hardworking mother Abigail O'Hurley Rockwell finally meets a man she can trust...but she's forced to deceive him to protect her sons.

Dance to the Piper—July
Broadway hoofer Maddy O'Hurley easily lands a plum role, but it takes some fancy footwork to win the man of her dreams.

Skin Deep—September
Hollywood goddess Chantel O'Hurley remains deliberately icy...until she melts in the arms of the man she'd love to hate.

Look for THE O'HURLEYS! And join the excitement of Silhouette Special Edition!

SSE451-1